EROMENOS

Eromenos
Melanie McDonald
© Melanie McDonald 2011
www.melaniejmcdonald.com

Seriously Good Books
Naples, Florida USA
www.seriouslygoodbooks.net

ISBN: 978–0–9831554–0–9

Cover and interior design by Ellery Harvey
Cover photo @ 2009 Megan Chapman
www.meganchapman.com
Map courtesy of U.S. Military Academy Archives

Cataloging-in-Publication Data
      McDonald, Melanie.
      Eromenos / Melanie McDonald. —1st ed.
      p. cm.
      1. Antinous, ca. 110-130—Fiction.
      2. Hadrian, Emperor of Rome, 76-138—Fiction.
      3. Favorites, Royal—Rome—Fiction.
      4. Emperors—Rome—Fiction.
      5. Rome—History—Hadrian, 117-138—Fiction.
      I. Title.

PS3563.A2345E76 2011
813'6--dc22

First edition, 2011

EROMENOS

MELANIE McDONALD

• SERIOUSLY GOOD BOOKS •

For Kevin

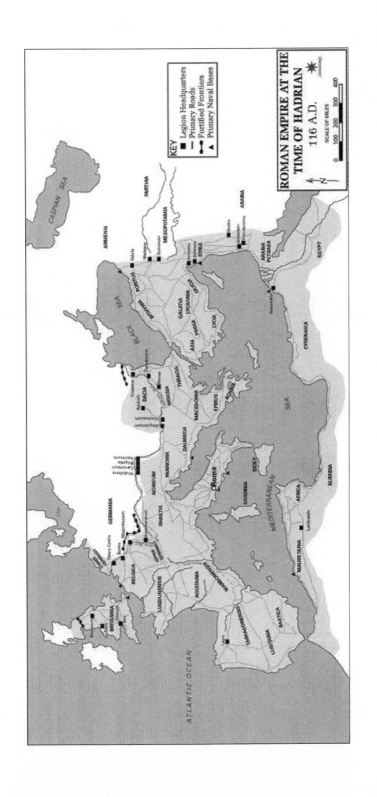

I hate and I love. Why, you might ask.

I don't know. But I feel it happening and I hurt.

—Catullus 85

PROLOGUE

SUCH A QUIET NIGHT, after Alexandria. I can hear the wild dogs barking along the banks outside Hermopolis, where the imperial fleet lies anchored. Farther down, ibis and river horse alike doze hidden among reeds beneath the turning wheel of constellations. The moon itself is dark, an auspicious sign for my purposes.

Here in our quarters, the only other soul awake is the guard on watch. Should he come round to check, these words are safe—he cannot read Greek. These last four nights, while the empire sleeps, I have assigned myself this confession. Any struggle must be resolved here upon these sheets, so the morrow holds nothing but acceptance, acquiescence, peace. With this lamp as witness I record my life until now. When I am finished, I must consign it all, save the final chapter, to the temple fire.

Earth, air, fire, water—all elements must be in accord for Our Lady to accept my offering for Hadrian's genius. That confluence of elements approaches.

EARTH

I. EARTH

I WAS BORN in Bithynia, in the town of Claudiopolis, during the reign of Trajan, and named Parthenos Antinous.

I have often wondered why my father and mother chose to name me after the foremost rejected suitor in the story of the *Odyssey*, killed with an arrow loosed by Odysseus; the shaft pierced his throat, leaving him to gag and choke while the life gushed out of him. Then again, Mantineia in Arcadia, Greek mother-city to our little town, was said to be founded by the princess Antinöe, guided to its site by a dragon. My name might be descended from hers. Whatever the reason for their choice, my parents carried it away with them into silence. My grandparents must not have known, for they never mentioned it.

My grandfather, Parthenos Philemon, made his fortune through shrewd land negotiations, while retaining the habits and attitude of a small-holdings farmer. He took care to teach me how our Greek forebears invented civilization, government, culture; how the Romans modeled their society on our own, and how our philosophy, medicine, arts and letters remain superior.

From my father's mother, a tiny, hawk-faced woman, I learned all the old Greek stories, as well as our local beliefs and superstitions. Every mountain, wood and stream belonged to a particular deity, and she claimed the river Sangarius was the birthplace of Dionysos. She said my grandfather was named for a man in ancient times who, alone out of an entire village, offered hospitality to strangers who were gods in disguise. Afterward, that ancient Philemon and his wife saw everyone and everything they loved vanish, destroyed beneath flood waters called forth by the gods, except for their own house, which became a temple.

She also told me how butterflies, those scraps of color that feather the meadows each spring, represent the souls of the departed, a concept known to philosophers as transmigration. Each year I watched when they appeared again, and always chose the most beautiful, a delicate blue, to be my mother.

My mother died in childbed before I turned four, but I remember her: lovely, kind, rather unhappy. Her name was Iris, after the goddess of the rainbow. I'm told she was intelligent, for a woman. From her I inherited certain physical characteristics more evocative of Asia than Greece; my broad face, high cheekbones, and deep eyes all disavow the Hellenic purity of my father's lineage.

As for my father, Parthenos Erythros, a surveyor and veteran of the Dacian wars fought during Trajan's reign, he was to be the heir, but his early death diverted the family properties into the care of his younger brother, Thersites. Though my father emphasized the superiority of Greek culture, he also took pride in the engineering feats accomplished by the Roman government. The imperial roads and aqueducts offered a vast improvement in living standards, especially for those in small towns.

My family grazed its herds on a hillside just south of the great evergreen forest that supplied timber for the shipbuilders of the province. Once when I was no older than five, on an outing with my father to this place, he directed my attention down valley to the long outline of the aqueduct, the arched stone flanks marching off to span the next hillside and carry on into the blue distance. The sun sat low in the sky, a tarnished disc of copper.

"Look, son," he said. "All of the water at our house comes from right there. Because of that aqueduct, no one has to carry heavy buckets of water just to be able to drink and bathe and wash any more, like people used to a long time ago."

He spoke that day of the precision of the grades implemented in the construction of those duct systems, a precision that assures the water always flows, uphill and down, from one town to the next. Like water through the aqueduct, his amazement conveyed itself to me.

"I promise you, Antinous, that aqueduct will outlast its builders until the next ten generations of Romans have passed, at least."

Standing at his side there on the hill, my childish mind conjured an image of this line of succession of which he spoke—a legion of men whose sons, grandsons and further descendants all stood stacked atop each other's shoulders, forming a human ladder like the tumblers in the market square might make. The ladder in my mind stretched up toward the sun, its topmost forms invisible against the zenith's brightness.

Despite illustrious ancestry and potential posterity, I grew up a small town boy, provincial and ignorant in manners and outlook. I spent much of my early childhood outdoors, herding, hunting, and observing nature, whose lessons, sensuous and cruel, she offers to any who wish to sit at her feet. I hugged those lessons to myself and pondered them in solitude, long before the years of my formal education began.

When I was six, wandering about in the cook's garden behind our villa, I discovered a field mouse dead in a thicket of berry brambles as high as my waist. Gazing at those translucent claws, his fur the color of bark and stone, I wondered how he came to be suspended there between earth and sky, like a tiny Antaeus. Maybe he had climbed up to escape one of our cats or wriggled loose from the talons of a hawk or owl only to drop down and become entangled in those thorns he mistook for his salvation. Perhaps he had been summoned there by Apollo Smynthius, Lord of field mice and the plague, my favorite god in the story of the Greek war against the Trojans.

Studying the creature's unnatural position, my wonder turned to pity, for death had left him in a state of indignity. Heedless of the bramble spines that scored my forearms, I reached into the thicket to dislodge him, an effort frustrated by the clumsiness of my childish fingers. I carried him away and deposited him on solid ground at last beneath a rosebush, where his tiny stink bothered no one as he returned to the soil.

I wondered if mice went to Hades, and imagined their tiny shades scrabbling about among the tall ones of famous men.

Then I went into the kitchen and washed my hands of him like a good boy.

The cook rewarded my compassion with a spoonful of honey to pour out as the mouse's libation. She had myriad ways of skimming from the larder: a spoon of honey here, there a bladeful of expensive spice that disappeared into the folds of her robes. She must have known I was not one to tell. I thought it only fair that the one who prepared all the food for our household also sample it herself.

Another time, at the age of nine, I set off alone to tend a herd of my grandfather's goats. Their self-congratulatory rubbing against trees and hedgerows left clots of greasy wool behind to stir in the breeze. I thought about how the cook converted their milk into a delicious crumbly white cheese. Rambling after them over the hillside, I heard a keening, and followed it into a copse, where I discovered a fox caught by its forelegs in a snare. Two crows had come to peck at its eyes.

I pulled my slingshot from my belt and grabbed a stone to fire at the birds. They retreated to a nearby tree, cawing at my intrusion.

The blinded fox's cries softened to a whimper after its tormentors had gone. When it heard my soft approach on foot it scrabbled with its hind paws, trying in vain to get a purchase on the leafy ground and yank itself free to escape this new threat.

Up close, I smelled the metal tang of blood overlying the creature's own musky odor. I knocked it in the head with a large stick. Then, to be sure, wrapped my slingshot around its muzzle, pulled aside the white ruff, and slit its throat with my knife.

I sliced through the rope and freed its forelegs, which it had begun to gnaw in its bid for freedom, and laid the fox on the ground below the trap. I thought of taking the pelt, or perhaps just the tail, that gaudy flame, but couldn't bear to mutilate the corpse further. The unknown hunter could have it to pay for his ruined rope.

The crows, with the prudence of their species, had flown away by then, or I would have killed them as well.

That day I made a vow to myself, never to betray any weakness of my own to an enemy if it lay at all within my power to conceal it. Long before I began to study philosophy, such encounters with natural cruelty had already encouraged in me a certain tendency toward secrecy and stoicism.

Soon after that incident, my father died. I came in one evening after bringing our small herd of goats back down to the paddock for milking to find my grandparents seated together on a couch in our villa, silent. My grandmother's face bore traces of tears. They told me my father's body had been carried home from the site of a new road project for the province. That was where he had suddenly slumped over the groma he was using to mark a sight line. His contorted face at first went pale and clammy, then flooded with color before his breath stopped.

The engineer who brought home his body returned later that evening with his equipment. My father's sundial they placed in the atrium. His groma disappeared into a chest for safekeeping. Perhaps my grandmother thought I might use it someday if I chose to follow his path and become a surveyor myself. He and I had, after all, shared a fascination with aqueducts and arches, bridges and tunnels, though his interest was based on professional knowledge of their construction, mine on imagination and wonder.

His bust soon joined my mother's in the foyer of the atrium, where our lares were worshipped. My grandparents let me take charge of making the household offerings at that time. I grieved for him, or rather for my own loss of him, but found solace in the woods and on the hillsides. The solitude of those places felt as familiar as our own hearth.

In the years following, I learned to hunt and to fish and to set snares for small game, although I preferred tracking animals to killing them. I found and tamed so many tortoises, hares, baby birds, squirrels and hedgehogs that my grandmother eventually forbade me to bring another living creature home from the woods.

I spent a great deal of time studying animals, creeping as close to them as possible for my observations. I cultivated an ability to find a spot, remain still and quiet, and disappear into the surroundings, so that the creatures of the wood carried on their routines, ignoring my presence. I felt blessed by Artemis when a doe nudged her twin fawns onto their feet and led them right past me to another section of the wood where the acorns lay thicker on the ground. They passed so close, I could have stroked those spotted hides had I reached forth a hand. On another occasion, I saw a bird dragging its wing along the ground just in front of me, as if to lure me toward herself; she had hatchlings in a nest nearby, and meant to offer herself as a sacrifice, if necessary, to protect them.

During the first decade of my life, my child-mind absorbed knowledge with the greed of a beggar who gobbles a banquet, and disgorged that knowledge just as readily. Would that I had learned the rudiments of mathematics with such an eager mind. (Much later, I set myself to study it, and expended great effort to grasp its tenets, with little success.)

An earthquake struck Bithynia in my eleventh year. I remember the ground rippled like the skin over a dog's haunch when he feels aggravated by fleas. Although the tremors devastated Nikomedia on the coast, and other parts of the province, our own town withstood the earth's shudders. A few cracks appeared in the columns of the temple of Mercury, where doctors and thieves all sacrifice. One eyewitness reported seeing the serpents entwined on the caduceus of the god's statue writhe and tremble of their own accord. That seemed to be the worst of it. Our greatest damage at home occurred when my grandmother's favorite bowl leaped from its shelf and crashed into a thousand shards on the tile floor.

My grandfather made a visit to Nikomedia soon afterward to check on several friends and to assess the damage there for himself. He found his friends, and indeed most of the residents, to be in good spirits, but unsure how long it might take for the city to reconstruct itself. Nikomedia, as Pliny the Younger once observed, was known for excessive squabbling in local politics and a lack of coherent planning and building programs. That city's difficulties in rebuilding after the quake seemed to bear out the truth of his allegations.

As I continued into the second decade of life, the earthquake that is adolescence caused my body to change in various ways. I grew taller and slimmer, the pudginess of childhood melting from my fingers, knees and middle. New sensations that came on in the night perplexed me. The planes of my face were changing, though I didn't realize or care; it never occurred to me to study my own features in the mirror. (Such vanity, like primping, seemed the prerogative of girls.) Instead, I took pride in the strength of new muscle and sinew in my legs and arms. My grandfather laughed whenever I flexed my biceps, showing off, and my grandmother fussed over my clothing, complaining that I outgrew my tunics faster than she could sew them.

Certain people of my acquaintance looked upon me with new interest. When I accompanied my grandfather to the baths, men who never acknowledged my presence now spoke to me, asking how school or music lessons were going, or complimented my grandfather on his "fine boy" right in front of me. My family and our servants, however, still treated me in much the same manner as they always had. Since they made no fuss about my changing looks, I took no great interest in them myself. I am ashamed to say that later on at court I sometimes succumbed to the temptations of vanity, due to the attention I received. As I aged, I grew wiser about appearances, and warier of flattery. Beauty, a gift from the gods, soon enough becomes its own curse.

THE YEAR I turned twelve, my grandfather announced I would be sent to stay with a friend of the family in Nikomedia in order to continue my studies. I felt sad to leave the countryside I loved, but looked forward to the trip to the coast, and obeyed him without complaint. I didn't know the particulars of the arrangement between my grandfather and his friend Deucalion, a ship builder and horse breeder, but understood my prospects could only improve with the opportunity for further education, in a coastal town with more resources than our village offered.

On the day I left home, I bundled my tunics, my school books, my slingshot, knife, bow and quiver full of arrows into my trunk and dragged it to the atrium, where my grandfather waited to help me load it onto the oxcart and my grandmother waited to kiss me goodbye.

As we traveled west over the ridge road, a sudden tang of salt became noticeable in the breeze that stirred the hairs on the oxen's ears and lifted the edges of our tunics. When I mentioned this smell to my grandfather, he said, "That, Antinous, is the smell of the sea."

We arrived in Nikomedia and found our way to the ship builder's villa through a maze of streets bustling with commerce, raucous with the ring and clatter of axes and hammers and shriek of seagulls.

Deucalion, a stocky man of swarthy complexion, greeted my grandfather with affection and then turned his attention to me, where I stood waiting beside my trunk of belongings. Studying my features in a manner that seemed brusque, yet not unkind, he said to my grandfather, "Ah, yes. This one can't stay buried forever."

He offered us a simple but delicious meal of fish, bread, and figs. Afterward one of his servants helped me unpack and settle in while he and my grandfather visited and caught up on local news and gossip. I overheard Deucalion say in jest of a mutual friend, known to be fond of his wine, "His liver has suffered more torments than Prometheus's." My grandfather laughed, but made no reply I could catch.

When the time came for my grandfather to take his leave, I knew by the tilt of his chin that I had made a good impression on my host, and that my welcome there in Deucalion's house was genuine.

My room, while larger than my old room at home, was just as spare in its accoutrements, which suited me, lacking in possessions as I was in those days. My host's family, with whom I soon became acquainted, included his blonde wife, Melita, and his brown-haired daughter, Penelope, whose husband, an engineer, had been called up to the northern frontier of Britannia to help construct a wall ordered by Emperor Hadrian for protection against barbarian tribes. He was expected to be gone for another couple of years at least. Mother and daughter spent much of their time together, running the household with the servants, baking their renowned honey-sesame seed cakes for sacrificial offerings, and visiting with the neighbor women, one of whom Deucalion declared a peerless spy and gossip.

"Give no heed to rumors, Antinous," he said to me one night at dinner, after Melita repeated the woman's latest scurrilous report about some other of their neighbors. "I can assure you, if you spend even a moment worrying what some dried-up old pig slit might say about you, you'll not travel far in this world."

Deucalion's shipyard and his stable both fascinated me. When I wasn't in school, I divided my time between the two. The shipyard reeked of pine resin, hot tar, and rotten fish, the air salted with the curses and laughter of seafaring men. I watched as the workers assembled ship skeletons from a vast pile of lumber harvested from the Arcadian forests, covered them with wooden planks, treated them with pitch to make them seaworthy, and then assembled lattices of riggings after hoisting tall posts, each a single pine trunk, for the vessels' main sails. I wondered whether I might ever sail on such a ship.

"The Romans build their ships all backwards," Deucalion once said to me. "Instead of building the frame first and then covering it, they construct the outside of the hull, then reinforce its insides. How they ever keep those old gut buckets afloat is beyond me."

He knew his own business, but I thought the Roman triremes I'd seen in port looked much sleeker than the sturdy merchant ships in which he specialized.

Staring out at the harbor where gulls mewled and dove that afternoon, I imagined Icarus taking leave of earth to soar above the bright water, climbing against the face of the sun until the wax began to give, his tunic fluttering in the feather-strewn wind while he dropped through the air and splashed down.

THE STABLE, WHICH also smelled unbearable at first, held even more fascination for me, a boy who yearned to ride. As a novice, I was indulged to a degree that I only now appreciate, with lessons from both my host and his stable hand, nicknamed Hephaestus, while I progressed from the oldest and tamest horse of the herd to the most spirited.

Those dozen or so horses in the stable required the full-time care of Hephaestus. Though a young man, no more than thirty, he walked with a limp. He'd been thrown from a horse he tried to break too soon after its arrival from the Sangarius river valley, leaving him saddled with a broken hip and a nickname. From Hephaestus I first learned how some Celts and Gauls in the north make cunning shoes of metal for their horses, attaching them to their hooves with iron nails.

"The weather up there is so damp, they must protect them somehow, else they're liable to soften and rot," he said, shaking his head at their ingenuity. "Don't seem to bother the horses any. There's no feeling in the hard part of the hooves where the nails go in. The shoes are little half-moons that fit around the hoof-rim. And that iron wears and wears, much longer than leather bindings."

Listening to his story, trying to picture such devices in my mind, I wondered whether someday I might visit Gaul, or the barbarian lands further north near the new imperial wall, perhaps upon a horse whose shoes outnumbered mine. Such was the fabric of my boyish dreams and fancies in those days. I had no premonition that my fate approached in the form of the ruler sailing toward us over the western horizon.

SO WE MET, in that city where the earth moved, when I was twelve. Awed before the god-man who trailed the glory of Empire behind him, I could no more bring myself to look full into his face than to stare into the noonday sun. But the day we met was not the first time I ever saw Hadrian. Three days earlier, my schoolmate Patrius and I snuck away from our afternoon lessons and hid in some bushes along the road outside Nikomedia to watch the imperial entourage arrive. We wanted to be the first to see it. Everyone in that scrubbed and flower-bestrewn town had turned out in their grandest finery to welcome the emperor. All anticipated a spectacle, and were not disappointed.

Every horse and rider flashed red, black, and white, with gold trimmings abundant as the saffron blooming in the hills. The royal standard swayed aloft in time to martial accompaniment. A whiff of expensive horseflesh reached us when those beauties pranced by, bright hooves clattering on the paving stones. Even my untrained eye could pick out musculature that proved descent from bloodlines far superior to those of my host's horses, which had seemed excellent to me until that day. I wondered how it must feel to ride such a creature.

Then he appeared before us. Emperor Hadrian, draped in purple and commanding a spirited mount, might have been Zeus himself come down from Olympus, though he arrived sunburnt and bareheaded as the Divine Julius. His beard, which lent him the appearance of a Greek philosopher, covered an old scar, as I later discovered. Hadrian, like my own father, fought in the Dacian wars, but this imperial apparition before us appeared to hold little else in common with a mortal like my late father. I stared and stared, yet could not get my eyes full. Who might have predicted on that day how well I should come to know that all-too-human man on parade. Ganymede, I imagine, suspected nothing when the eagle first descended.

Local officials, aware of the emperor's proclivities and appreciation for beauty, had invited all the attractive youths and young men in the province to attend various events planned in the emperor's honor. I attended a reading at the palace where Julius once yielded himself to King Nikomede II in return for a fleet of warships and earned himself the sobriquet "Queen of Bithynia" for his acquiescence.

Though I felt too shy to look at the emperor while local poets declaimed their work, I knew whenever the imperial gaze followed me. I moved with deliberation about the room, always aware of his attention. I tried to focus on the festivities, yet my mind grew distracted. I felt far too intimidated, even after my inclusion in that select group, to attempt to address him myself.

Instead, he took the initiative. Hadrian, ruler of the Roman Empire, deigned to speak to a boy from the backwater province of Bithynia, and asked if I was enjoying myself. His voice was bathed in honey. I blushed and stammered in reply. To quote Socrates, that day my soul sprouted feathers, took wing.

All during the rest of his tour of the city, I followed the news and gossip about his various stops. He visited the library and the baths, talked with people at the market, and inspected the damage lingering from the earthquake, which prompted the local officials to claim inadequate funding to justify the lack of rebuilding efforts to date. The emperor promised increased financial assistance, but in return, demanded more control over local projects.

Hadrian also made a point of finding time to visit Deucalion's shipyard. Deucalion, of course, extended an invitation for the emperor to dine with the family and some friends at the villa.

The day of the imperial dinner party, the entire household whirled in a frenzy of shopping, cleaning, polishing, cooking, and preening. The finest fish, oysters, and eels were procured from the market, the most august wine brought up from the cellar. Melita, overwhelmed, retired to her quarters with a headache early that afternoon, leaving the rest of the details of the feast's preparation to her daughter Penelope, her housekeeper, and her cook.

That evening Emperor Hadrian complimented the master and mistress on their lovely home and hospitality. He enquired after Penelope's husband and provided her with an update on the northern wall construction project. He queried me about my own family and hometown, and then discoursed about horses with Deucalion, graciously including me in the conversation as if I, too, were a seasoned judge and breeder of fine flesh. The emperor even grew relaxed enough to tell a funny story on himself.

"We were traveling light through the countryside one afternoon, in a hurry to reach the river and set up camp by nightfall, when a local woman appeared, seeking to petition me right there in the middle of the road. I waved her off, saying I didn't have time, and we kept riding on. After which came her cry of disgust: 'Cease to be Caesar, then.'"

He and Deucalion laughed while the two women of the house looked at each other wide-eyed over the peasant woman's effrontery.

Hadrian continued.

"So I dismounted and heard her out, then sent a suggestion to the local proconsul for resolving her boundary dispute with a neighbor. She thanked me with great dignity and a stab at formal Latin. It took all my fortitude to keep from exploding with laughter. I never would have offended her, after her temerity."

Watching him talk, I discovered that his eyes, with their penetrating gaze, were not brown as I earlier thought, but a changeable grey-blue, and full of the light lent to men's eyes by intelligence. While he discoursed, I permitted myself to study his features with impunity, delighted by such an opportunity to observe the emperor up close and at his ease.

In the course of that evening, Hadrian mentioned a lodge he owned in the forests near the Sangarius river, and suggested he might invite us to come along there sometime to hunt. I felt both excited and frightened by the prospect of such an imperial outing.

His own visit was later dissected and studied at the baths with everyone else in town. Deucalion's friends and neighbors professed amazement over the emperor's attentions to me, and how obvious he'd made it that I caught his eye.

"You'll be summoned to join that fine school of his in Rome, Antinous. You will, just wait," said Patrius, my friend who hid with me to watch Emperor Hadrian come to town. His voice now held admiration fringed with envy. I demurred, as manners required, but hoped in secret it might be so. The imperial paedagogium in Rome trained young men for service in the imperial retinue and household, and also prepared them for an eventual career in civil service. Rumor held that its ranks served Hadrian as a harem as well, a function more shadowy than defined in my understanding at the time. The emperor was known to admire Greek culture. I hoped that affinity for my heritage might increase whatever chance I possessed as a candidate for his school. I also wondered if my Greek heritage could make up for the fact that I was no patrician.

The summons to Rome arrived two months later. It was addressed to me in care of my host and sealed with the emperor's signet embedded in a thin rosette of red wax. The imperial missive possessed a rare air, one of elegance and command.

Deucalion, in a gesture of respect, handed it on to me to open, although by right as my temporary guardian he could have done so himself. The messenger who delivered it stood by, waiting for me to read the enclosed invitation and then give my reply.

I felt reluctant, almost afraid to break open that beautiful seal and vouchsafe the contents it concealed. I knew that as soon as I did, my life would change forever. Despite the late afternoon sun radiating heat into the atrium, I found myself shivering.

I used one finger and tried to pry his mark intact from the edge of the sheet, thinking to preserve it for a keepsake—but even that gentle pressure caused it to crack and shatter, damaged beyond recovery. I unrolled the summons and read the message inscribed in a beautiful hand on papyrus of the finest quality.

"Imperator Caesar Trajan Hadrian Augustus, son of the deified Trajan Parthicus, grandson of the deified Nerva, Pontifex Maximus of Tribunician Power for six years, Consul for the third time, to the young citizen Parthenos Antinous of the Bithynian Province, his guardian Kalios Deucalion of Nikomedia and his family, greetings.

"Having made acquaintance with you upon my sojourn in Nikomedia, and having further developed that acquaintance under the auspices of Deucalion while enjoying the hospitality offered by his lovely wife Melita in their gracious home, I am pleased to offer you,

Antinous, a term of residency as a student at the Imperial Paedagogium in Rome, as well as the position of groom and page in service of the Royal Court at Rome.

"I look forward to the pleasure of your response. Transportation to Rome will be arranged for you within a month upon acceptance of this proffered appointment.

"Farewell. September 6, from Smyrna"

Deucalion sent word to my grandparents of the emperor's invitation. Any necessary permission was granted, and they planned to arrive within a week to say goodbye and see me off to Rome. My daydream of sailing the wine-dark sea on a ship like one of Deucalion's now verged on reality.

THE WEATHER AT sea held clear for my journey to Rome that fall. I felt fortunate not to succumb to sea sickness, as did some other passengers aboard the *Nereid*, a merchant vessel that had been requisitioned to pick up luxury goods including silk and spices at various ports along the coast, as well as a few passengers who were, like me, on official business of the Empire.

When we sailed south into the Aegean, the pines straggling along down the coast began to give way to olive trees, gnarled forms like old men wrapped in grey-green mantles clinging to the shoreline, braced against the wind. The white rock outcroppings along the bluffs gleamed in the sunlight like the bones of drowned men.

My needs while aboard were looked after by Periander, a galley slave whose services were thus engaged for the duration of the trip. Periander, the youngest hand on board at age twelve himself, seemed more of a pet or mascot to the rest of the crew, and he informed me that the owner of the ship also owned all of them, including Periander's own master, a sailor who had bought him from his parents in Syria for a few dozen sestertii, as if he were a parrot or a baboon. He made a pallet for me on deck each night, since the weather held clear, so that I might sleep beneath the stars. He looked so longingly at the sausages and other foods he cooked for me in the galley that I always ended up sharing part of my dinner with him.

"Boy, stop loafing and grab that line," one of the crewmen shouted once while Periander stood talking to me on deck. No sooner had he got hold of the line as instructed than another sailor yelled, out of contrariness, "Peri, toss me back that bolt there, by your feet."

Periander gave an exaggerated sigh and rolled his eyes.

"Castor and Pollux preserve us," he said. "Watch this, Ant."

Without letting go of the rope he held in both hands, with bare toes agile as a monkey's he nipped up the little metal cylinder that lay on the board beside his left foot and pitched it at the second man, evoking a volley of laughter and whistles all around. The crewmen all were well pleased with such exhibits of agility, showing off their pet's tricks to entertain the passengers. Meanwhile, Periander, touching in his eagerness to befriend me, talked, pranced, cajoled, teased, and showed off his own cache of tricks, sleights of hand taught to him by various members of the crew, capering about like a faun of Pan transported to the realm of Oceanus.

Periander's right elbow reposed at a grotesque angle, having healed that way after an injury. When I asked what happened, thinking he must have fallen from the mast pole or undergone some other accident on board, Periander shrugged, looked away, then looked me in the eye and said, "Broke it. My dad."

I only now realize what Periander, the slave of a slave, must have endured within the awful confines of that ship, and with what grace and wit, a born survivor. I wonder what Hadrian might have made of him. At the time, however, I remained far too naïve to perceive his circumstances. The ship's crew treated me with civility, even deference, for already the aura of empire had cast around me a mantle of safety none dared to breach.

Once we passed beyond mainland Greece, heading out of the Aegean into the Mediterranean, we recalled the events of Odysseus's journey, and wondered whether we might be passing those lands where he and his crew encountered the lotus-eaters, the Cyclops, Circe, and Calypso, while their ships managed to escape both Scylla and Charybdis.

Poseidon bore no grudge against our own ship's captain or crew. No sirens waylaid us, and with the help of Zephyrus we soon passed Sicily and hove into port at Ostia, south of Rome. There, the captain gave thanks to Portuna astride his dolphin with an offering of honey cakes and wine.

Periander begged me not to go ashore, to stay on board.

"Don't go to that old school, Antinous. Stay here. Stow away and hide until we cast off again. We'll jump ship next port, you and I, sail to Africa. It'll be a grand life. We can search for treasure, hunt wild animals, go fight pirates—"

I shook my head. "Pompey got rid of all the pirates hundreds of years ago."

"Then we'll be pirates," Periander said.

"I can't. They're expecting me, and besides, what will you tell the emperor's courier? You'll have to lie."

"No, I won't," he said, and sliced me with a smile like a knife. "I'll just push you overboard and tell him you fell into the sea."

THERE ON THE dock at Ostia I was greeted by a servant from the palace. He wore linen finer than I had ever worn. My new toga with its purple stripe—a parting gift from my grandfather—seemed shabby by comparison. Soon enough, though, I would find myself garbed in tunics of even finer quality, the costume of a court page.

While we waited on the dock for my trunk to be carried off the ship and then loaded onto the imperial barge, I waved goodbye to Periander, still on deck. He scowled, made a rude gesture with one hand, and turned his back on me for good. I hoped my imperial escort hadn't noticed that exchange.

As a guest of the emperor, I was spared the usual necessity of an inventory of my belongings by the customs officers waiting to collect import fees from passengers who disembarked dockside. Trunk stowed at last, with the smell of the sea in my nostrils still, I felt both frightened and exhilarated by whatever new experiences might now lie in wait ahead, a reality I could not even begin to conceive, and my gaze turned inland once my escort and I stepped into the river craft that carried us on an anabasis via the Tiber into the waiting arms of that mistress of the world, Rome herself, eternal city.

AIR

II. Air

ROME LOOMED LARGER than I had imagined. Its circus and amphitheatre, white marble temples, palaces, libraries, and the public edifices around the forum rose above the throngs of people (many of them poor, hungry, and desperate) who crowd the city's streets all day and cause an unending cacophony in its thoroughfares.

Except for those wealthy few whose mansions and villas, wreathed about with pleasure gardens, recline upon the surrounding hills, most of the city's inhabitants dwell in apartment complexes rising like hives full of honeycomb, and likewise buzzing with activity all of the time. Shoddy construction and cheap materials cause frequent conflagrations, since whenever one apartment catches fire, those surrounding it go up as well, and often take adjacent buildings with them, taxing the city's firemen to the limits of their strength and available resources. At first it seemed surprising how often smoke soiled the air, or blazes lit the nighttime skyline, illuminating the tangle of carts forbidden to traverse the streets on business by daylight, but no one else ever seemed panicked by these incidents, and soon I also learned to ignore them.

We new arrivals at the imperial paedagogium had been given a few days to be introduced at the palace, settle into our own quarters, and acquaint ourselves at the school before we were allowed to go off on our own to explore the great city sprawled like a wanton across the seven hills, and proclaimed eternal by Emperor Hadrian himself.

Senses engorged by new sights, sounds, smells and tastes, I meandered along her streets, visited the various quarters of the metropolis and sampled the wares of merchants whose offerings represented all the riches of the far-flung empire right there in its pulsating heart. Everything is available in Rome, if only you agree to the price: Queen Money, to quote Horace, rules all.

The hawking of street vendors competed with curses flung by pedestrians, braying mules, hammers on anvils, mourners hired to wail after funeral processions, cymbals and drums punctuating religious celebrations, barking dogs, tavern patrons, crying babies and screaming children, robbery victims shouting at pickpockets, fullers singing at their work, and detachments of army recruits on parade through the middle of the street, the hobnails of their boots clanging against the paving stones. And beneath those stones, under the feet of the multitudes, the Cloaca Maxima, a vast sewer main that flows beneath the city like the dark twin of the Tiber.

On game days the spectators at the Flavian amphitheatre, almost seventy thousand strong, take in the sights of gladiators at battle, of exotic animals such as lions, tigers, giraffes, elephants, ostriches, and rhinos exhibited and slaughtered by the droves, and of various horse and chariot races. I was told the shouting of the crowds on such days could be heard far off in the countryside, sounding almost as if they were calling the hogs that root for acorns in the woods beyond the rustic farmlands. The chariot races and other events at the Circus Maximus drew even larger mobs, for the circus can hold almost four hundred thousand souls.

At the site where Caesar was assassinated, I noticed a large number of cats always lounging about, as if in hopes of communication with the great man's spirit. Befriended by a few of these strays, I gave ten sestertii to the priest at a nearby shrine of Isis, for he had taken it upon himself to be sure these local denizens, sacred to the goddess, always had food and water.

Each time I passed the temple of Vesta with its eternal flame, and the house of her consecrated virgins, I recalled the story of a Vestal virgin who consorted with a man, breaking her vow to the goddess. Upon being discovered, she was buried alive, upside down—a punishment deemed appropriate for her sacrilege. Her consort was merely whipped to death.

In the multi-storied market halls of Trajan's Forum, people of every nationality appeared, and during each visit I saw clothing, jewelry, and hairstyles such as I never dreamed of back home. Some of the more extravagant merchants displayed custom-made mosaics of the items they purveyed. Captivated by these tile images, I decided to seek out the particular artist whose designs I found most colorful. From him, I commissioned a mosaic featuring a ship to send to Deucalion, in thanks for his many kindnesses while he hosted me in Nikomedia.

The variety of goods available at market every day, and the quality of the selections for those able to afford such purchases, astonished me: cheeses, olives, olive oil, thyme-scented honey gold in its comb, fruits, nuts, herbs, spices, wine, smoked fish, dried fish, silvery stringers of fresh-caught, fish sauce, eels, sausages, poultry, meats, game, and bread baked fresh each day from flour provided by the ocean of grain pouring in from Egypt, about eight thousand tons each week.

One might find furniture handmade by the best wood carvers and iron wrights in Italy; silks and brocade from China; linen, papyrus, cosmetics and perfume from Egypt; wools and finely tooled leather from Gaul; carved ebony and ivory from Africa, along with terra cotta and carved wooden figurines for making offerings or shrines. Slaves, horses, oxen and other domestic creatures were purchased in the livestock markets nearby. Even human hair, lustrous blue-black skeins sheared from the heads of Indians, might be bought and made up into wigs, for those whose own locks failed them.

The price of goods shocked me at first. A loaf of bread, a cup of wine, each cost a quarter of a sestertius, while a bath cost one sesterius—four times what men paid back home. A cheap prostitute, as I later learned, might charge half that. Soldiers earned up to twelve hundred sestertii a year, common workers maybe two or three sestertii per day—just enough to stay fed and bathed.

My favorite snack soon became a bowl of soup made from day-old bread stewed with grain, peas or beans, topped with olive oil and a palmful of rosemary, "queen of the garden," as the vendor proclaimed each time he added it. Most Roman citizens ate such soup or bread as their daily ration. I, however, ate so many strange new treats that my stomach began to strain against my imperial tunic and forced me to curb my appetite.

On an impulse one afternoon I used almost half a week's allowance from home to buy a length of silk in the fabric stalls for ten sestertii. Blue as the Argus-eyed peacock and shot through with fine gold thread, the color reminded me of my mother. I had a seamstress cut it up and then hem the little squares to create a set of hand cloths for my personal use. From then on, I always kept one tucked somewhere in the folds of my outer garment.

I soon grew fond of visiting the spice quarter upstairs at the market, whose merchants traveled difficult land routes to and from the East to bring back frankincense, myrrh, ginger, turmeric, cloves, camphor, sandalwood, cardamom, sesame, cinnamon, and nutmeg, with a brown musty fragrance I particularly enjoyed. The exotic aromas offered a respite from the streets, which reeked of animal manure, fuller's urine, fish, rotted vegetables, the flung-out contents of chamber pots, and bodies and clothing too long unwashed. The three pepper sellers, Italians from the southern coast who sang at their work, always laughed to see me coming. Every time I drew near a display of their wares, I began to sneeze. At least I always had a cloth handy.

THE IMPERIAL PAEDAGOGIUM offered a curriculum intended to educate and finish young men as imperial pages and civil servants, but in truth we were a pack of beautiful boys, a seraglio of youths discovered and brought in from all over the empire.

The school itself was perched in Caput Africanae, a street hugging the Caelian Hill, and its facilities included classrooms, a library, living quarters both private and common, a gymnasium and training fields.

Our head master was a bald, thin-lipped freedman who took his duties seriously. He set a schedule that had us up by dawn, even though we might be required to stay out late into the night whenever royal banquets required our presence.

Mornings were spent studying philosophy, rhetoric, literature, mathematics, and geography, with music lessons twice a week before lunch. In the afternoons, we exercised, wrestled, trained with weapons, or competed in various athletic events. I noticed, in particular, one handsome older boy who excelled at archery. He was called Korias.

Those of us who served as grooms soon spent our early mornings and evenings before supper helping the stable master feed, exercise, bathe and brush the imperial horses. A pack of hunting dogs followed at our ankles and amused us with their antics while we made our rounds of the stables at the edge of the palace grounds.

The stable master, Momius, a grizzled old freedman with sun-squinted eyes, the rinds of his heels caked as often as not with manure, acted gruff toward new hands, impatient at any sign of laziness or carelessness with the animals. Yet his curses soon enough sounded like prayers to me, his way of calling down blessings around the horses and dogs and grooms left in his charge.

Momius knew the measure of every horse in Rome, knew which horse had won every race held for the last twenty years and from which bloodlines it descended. It was he who told me about the October Horse of Rome, a custom retained from the earliest days of the city.

"Every October," he said, "a race is held in the Forum during the festival of Jupiter Capitolinus. The winning horse is the sacrifice. Its head is cut off and displayed in a place of honor along the Sacred Way. The October horse protects the people of Rome for a year, until the next race, when its skull will be replaced by the head of its successor."

I spent many of my happiest hours out at the stables, engrossed in riding and caring for those creatures and watching while the hunt master worked the horses and the dogs, training them so their nerve could be counted upon to hold steady during the hunt. I hoped someday to be one of those grooms allowed to accompany the emperor and his friends when they rode out after stag or boar, or even bear or lion.

AT SCHOOL, ISSUES arising out of class and wealth differences sometimes caused conflicts within our ranks. Certain personalities also clashed on occasion. But many friendships and romances grew up there as well. In some cases, boys cemented bonds of fraternity with one another likely to endure for their lifetimes. Older boys often looked out for favorite younger ones, and helped with their acclimation to court life.

Early on, some of the other boys gave me a hard time for being Greek, a circumstance which no doubt I helped provoke with a youthful arrogance regarding my ancestral culture's superiority, despite the low social standing of my own family in comparison with many of theirs.

"If the Greeks were so advanced," one boy, a Roman patrician named Gracchus Lucius Marcus, asked me one day while several of us sat around talking together in the library, "why did they condemn Socrates to death? And

45

if he was so superior intellectually, why did he not write anything down?"

After a few such interrogations by Marcus and some others, I learned perhaps the most important lesson of all for surviving both in school and later at the court: Though the mind remains open, keep the mouth shut.

We new boys, shy at first, soon joined the others in discussions during our lessons and spent what free time we had in the school's new library, reading or studying between classes. We also spent time in the common dining area, where we took our meals on those evenings when no official banquets were held—that is, most evenings, since the emperor traveled for much of the year.

In the atrium, I studied the images of Rome's early heroes and heroines, and soon learned their stories. There were the founding twins, Romulus and Remus, suckled by a she-wolf, who reigned together until Romulus killed his brother and took over, as forecast by augurs. There was Lucretia, a virtuous woman spied upon and then raped by the son of Tarquin. Afterward, she killed herself in shame, spurring her Roman countrymen to defeat their Etruscan overlords and establish the Republic. (When I first met Empress Plotina, Hadrian's adoptive mother and the widow of his predecessor, Trajan, I felt struck by the similarity of her features and demeanor to that image of the noble woman who represented Roman honor.)

I also learned of Cincinnatus, a citizen appointed dictator in a time of war during the era of the Republic, who upon achieving the Roman victory renounced his title at once and retired to his farm outside the city. I found myself as moved by his story as when I first heard of Pheidippides' run from the plain of Marathon to relay the news of Athens' victory to its citizens. Just as men today still hark back to the ideals of Greek democracy, so too, I believe, will future generations of Romans continue to look back to the old Republic, and perhaps even to the current empire, though not to the reigns of those emperors corrupted by absolute power.

In the school's new library, some wag already had scratched bits of doggerel in one corner of the back wall, which I deciphered one morning for another new boy who couldn't yet read Latin: "Virgil is still the frog boy," "Pandora's jar was sealed up tight—Epimetheus pried. . ." and so forth, no doubt the handiwork of older students since none of us new boys would have dared leave our mark on the empire that way.

In the housing annex, we bunked in a wing with a dozen rooms. My room was far larger and much fancier than any back home, painted in shades of red, yellow, blue and black. It was carpeted with thick wool rugs, and furnished with cupboards, shelves, my own chest, and a table beside the bed, which was spread with embroidered linens and a heavy wool coverlet. Incense kept the air fragrant, and the lamps, braziers, and candles offered a wealth of light.

Back home, by habit I rose with the sun and went to bed soon after it set, so the early mornings didn't bother me at first. But there in the private quarters, one could stay up late into the night and read beneath those plentiful lights. So on many nights I chose books over sleep, until exhaustion caught up and I nodded off. The housemaid must have been the one who eased the book from my grasp, pulled the coverlet over me, and put out the light, for that was how I always woke. She also gave me a shy smile whenever we met in the hall.

A cook in the school's kitchen also took me under her care after I wandered into her corner of the place one day, looking for something to eat. She offered me pears, told me to feel welcome any time. Whenever I dropped by after that, she petted me and gave me choice morsels, and sometimes even fed me tales recalled from her own childhood, which I soon enough recognized as corrupted versions of Aesop's fables. I tried to show my gratitude in turn, bringing her flowers or spices from the market or collecting herbs for her from the imperial garden, but when she caught me washing out my own dirty cup and plate one afternoon after a snack during a free period, she looked bemused. No doubt she feared someone might see and think she'd set me to this menial task. She chided me, pretending an offense she perhaps did not feel.

"No, lad—I mean, sir," she said. "This is work for servants and women. You are a page of the imperial court now. You mustn't sully your hands with such tasks. Unless, of course, you go out hunting, or off to war."

She ruffled my hair, a gesture of affection my boyishness still allowed her back then, and sent me off to more appropriate diversions.

I still think of her and that maid with fondness, although I understand now what I did not as a child— their need, for their own dignity's sake, to observe the formalities proper to our separate stations in life. At home, servants always seemed part of the family to me. Circumstances were different at court.

EMPEROR HADRIAN HAD selected the palace built by Domitian, a complex of enormous rooms and mirrored galleries which occupied the Palatine hill, to use as his personal residence whenever he held court in Rome. At this palace, one of my first assignments as a new imperial page called for pouring the watered wine during feasts held for the emperor and his guests.

The opulence of the imperial banquet hall impressed me on first viewing, with its mosaics and enormous carpets, wall paintings with scenes of gods and goddesses at the hunt or at play, elegant tablecloths, silk-cushioned divans, silver, gold and cut-glass table service gleaming in the lamplight, but soon enough I became accustomed to it, as one does with any surroundings after a while, however humble or luxuriant. My focus turned instead to the performance of my official duties.

A senior page, the handsome archer named Demetrius Korias, volunteered to teach me the correct technique for the pouring of the wine and water. This involved grasping the handle of the flagon in a particular manner, and arching the wrist and forearm to minimize splashing.

"You'll notice," Korias said, "that by holding it this way, the curve of one's arm echoes the curve of the handle—a configuration considered graceful and pleasing to the eye, at least by the banquet steward." He grinned at me, his eyes full of mirth.

I felt quite nervous the first evening I served, but the various guests seemed kind, and several smiled as if for encouragement, or in recognition of my desire to please, and to execute my task without flaw. Not a drop fell awry, and I collapsed into bed later that night exhausted but happy to have acquitted myself well in the service of the emperor, even though, on that first night, I was not permitted to serve at Hadrian's own table. I noticed that Lucius Commodus, a young noble deemed worthy of consideration as the emperor's successor, was present at the emperor's table that evening, seated near Plotina, Hadrian's adoptive mother and the widow of Emperor Trajan. Later I learned that Commodus also was rumored to be the emperor's favorite among the court's young men.

At many of those banquets in my earliest days at court, I succumbed to gluttony, sampling all the exotica offered up for empire by wealth and power at those official feasts of greed. At times, it shames me now to say, I overindulged to the point of having to go and vomit. Such an endless profusion of delicacies seemed like nectar and ambrosia for a boy not from that city.

I ate hummingbird, thrush tongues, caviar, crayfish, artichokes, eels, peaches, oysters, snails, dormice, wild game, exotic fruits, and vegetables seasoned with expensive spices from India and China. The food was accompanied by the finest wines, Falernian, Nomentan, Setian, Amineum, and various other golden vintages from Campagna, Hispanica and Greece, sometimes served chilled by snow, transported to Rome at great cost to some banquet sponsor just for that purpose. In those dishes I devoured, I discovered even more of the world that still lay beyond my own experience, all offered up for the pleasure of the imperial court.

Yet after a while I noticed Emperor Hadrian himself did not always partake in these extravagances, despite being urged by those around him. He often preferred simpler dishes: grilled fish, or a bit of lamb, bread and olives, water and wine. Perhaps he had been offered so many delicacies that his palate, numbed by surfeit, craved the plain fare of his army years. Or perhaps one must become great before one's preferences are allowed to become so simple.

Hadrian, in his unique and unassailable position, felt no need for such exhibitions, I realize now, but tolerated them as a necessity for those beneath him, ceaseless in their efforts to impress and please him. And, too, perhaps we youths and beauties of the court, sleek partridges dressed in fine garments, were encouraged to desire the exotic, the rare, the savory, so that the great expense accrued and paid for such consumption, meant to promote various benefactors while they sought to curry favor with the emperor, might be justified. Power and wealth, I have learned, often exhibit themselves by such means.

As FOR MY schooling, I enjoyed the opportunity to read for myself those philosophers of whom I had so often heard from my father and grandfather, and the chance to discuss their works and ask questions of teachers whose intellects and ethics I respected. Rhetoric, Latin grammar and mathematics I did not enjoy, but persisted in those disciplines nonetheless.

When I had been at the court school for perhaps six months, Emperor Hadrian came to sit in and listen to our classes one afternoon, during the Ides of March, I believe. No doubt Hadrian felt it an appropriate day for Caesar to spend among schoolboys.

Because of the mild sunny weather, we sat outdoors that afternoon. Our teacher welcomed our royal visitor with a courteous speech and asked him to be seated. We were reading about Odysseus in a new Latin translation (which of course renamed him Ulysses), and had just been discussing his return to Ithaka in the guise of a beggar, and the beggar's odd request to participate in the archery contest for Penelope's hand, a contest which would soon reveal his deadly glory to the ill-fated suitors.

"Why a bow?" our teacher asked. "Why did the poet choose the bow—and Ulysses' own great bow, at that—as the weapon to be used in the contest for Penelope?"

"Because only he could string it," Marcus said, eager to show off, wanting to prove he had read the text and knew the answer.

"Yes, of course," said the teacher, with a bit of impatience, "we are told that in the text. But why a bow, rather than, let's say, a spear, or a sword?"

I understood what he was asking—what that weapon might represent symbolically, beyond a means to kill those rivals—but hesitated to volunteer an answer. The teacher saw the hesitation in my face, and called upon me anyway.

"Antinous, you looked as if you might have an idea."

"Sir," I said, "he might have chosen the bow and arrow since, traditionally, they are the weapons of the god of love, and Ulysses is competing to win his wife back from false lovers. The arrow flying into the rings is fairly obvious in its implications—"

A snicker, at once suppressed, interrupted my thought. Then the teacher said, "Yes, go on."

"And also—also." I took a breath. "Might it be because of the tension?"

"What do you mean, Antinous?"

"That tension which accompanies the stringing of the bow, which must be bent to receive it, and the drawing back of the arrow, the holding and then, release, the letting go.

"Because this scene is also full of tension. Those who know what soon will happen there in the banquet hall are taut with nerves. Penelope cries in the storeroom when she goes to retrieve his bow. Telemachus laughs, because he can't conceal his excitement over seeing his father in battle at last. Only Odysseus—Ulysses, I mean—holds his nerves in check. He remains in control even as he strings the bow, easy as a lyre, and plays it for and against the suitors."

I noted the lift of Hadrian's left eyebrow as he considered my answer.

"Well done, my boy," the teacher said. "I take it this is your favorite moment of his homecoming, for clearly you have given it some thought."

"Yes, sir," I said, "this, and the moment when his old dog knows him and thumps his tail in greeting."

"But isn't that a bit mawkish, sir?" Marcus, embarrassed earlier, now sought to regain face by making me wrong.

Then Hadrian spoke.

"It is a bit sentimental, I'm afraid." He glanced at Marcus, and at the teacher, and then at me. "And one of my favorite moments in the homecoming, as well."

"Thank you, sir," I said, then wondered if I should have spoken again at all. I felt the color rise and splash like blood across my own throat.

After class, walking through the courtyard, I looked up to see Korias above me in one of the oak trees. It seemed he had dawdled about in order to wait for me. He dropped down to the earth with a cat's grace when I drew near, and spoke to me.

"I liked what you said about the tension of the bow, how it correlated to the tension of the scene," he said. With a little jump, he sprang up and caught the tree limb above our heads, dangling from it by his hands for a moment before letting go again.

"I thought you might," I said. "You're an excellent archer yourself."

"Were you afraid to answer in front of the Emperor?" His eyes on me were guileless. Extraordinary eyes, amber irises ringed and flecked with green.

"Yes," I said. "But when the teacher called on me, I was more afraid not to."

Korias laughed and tossed an arm around my shoulders, a gesture that thrilled me with its calculated casualness, and began to steer me on across the courtyard.

Whatever else we may have talked about then, I now can no longer recollect. The usual silly schoolboy offerings, and back-and-forth banter of flirtation. While his beautiful lean body, hanging from that tree, had made my heart spring like a lamb in the meadow. I wanted, more than anything, to feel it pressed against me.

ONE DAY SOON afterward, a package arrived for me at school.

Emperor Hadrian had sent me a bracelet of hammered copper from one of his family's Spanish mines.

"The Emperor congratulates you for making excellent progress in your courses," said the palace slave who presented the gift box to me where I sat reading in one corner of the library.

I slipped the bracelet onto my wrist. It fit as if made for me. Perhaps it was. Then I asked the messenger who delivered it to wait for a moment, so that I might write a thank-you to convey my gratitude to the emperor as soon as possible.

I wasn't sure quite what to think of this gesture—perhaps every student received a similar token once it became clear he might be a suitable addition to the emperor's retinue.

After the servant departed with my note in hand, I turned the bracelet this way and that, studying it. I decided to stash it in my linen chest for safekeeping until I had a better idea of just what the gift and the wearing of it represented. Already I had seen how envy and competitiveness could turn some of the boys vicious, and I wanted to avoid trouble if possible. I planned to wait until our next audience with the emperor to wear it in public.

Several days later, despite my caution, a calamity struck. Marcus played a trick on me that took my breath with its mean-spiritedness. After class one morning, while some of us played at knucklebones and the others sat watching, or else stood around kicking a ball back and forth, Marcus walked up and said, "By the way, has anyone see my bracelet, the twisted silver one? I seem to have mislaid it—can't find it anywhere." He stooped and grabbed up the ball as it rolled past him, cradling it to his chest to maintain everyone's attention.

I knew the bracelet of which he spoke. In fact, I had complimented it earlier, and wondered whether it had been a gift to him from the emperor although, of course, I hadn't asked.

Everyone said no, they hadn't seen it, almost in unison. "No matter," he said, "I just wondered."

He dropped the ball and with a gesture of nonchalance kicked it to the next boy. He began to stroll away. Without looking back he said, "I'm sure it will turn up eventually."

Then, in the evening, just before we left our private quarters to go to supper, Marcus, who had been pacing around, called out, "Wait, everyone," so that we all turned in the hallway where we were lining up.

He paused beside my quarters and, when everyone's eyes found him, stepped in and pounced on an item amid the tumble of foolscap, twine, candle ends and other articles heaped atop the small table beside my bed. He held it aloft—the missing bracelet.

"Antinous, please explain," he said, looking me straight in the eye.

Staring at him across the empty space between us, I felt the blood rush into my face and then fall away to my feet, leaving me leaden. He had planted his own bracelet there on my night table to make it look as if I had stolen it. I knew any protest I made now would only make me look guiltier, and so remained silent.

"Really, if you wanted to borrow it, all you had to do was ask."

He smirked at me, his eyes narrowed.

Korias and the others, embarrassed by this scene, slipped away one by one until only Marcus and I remained. I still did not know what to say, what to do. Then an idea came to me.

"I'm sorry, Marcus," I said, in my most ingratiating voice. "Please allow me to make it up to you."

"How do you propose to do that?" He was enjoying himself, now that I was at his mercy.

I crossed the room to where he stood beside my bed. I bent down, opened my linen chest, and felt beneath my folded laundry. The copper bracelet still nestled where I had hidden it. I turned to my accuser and held it out to him.

"Here," I said. "Please accept this as a token of apology."

"And from whom did you steal this one?" He laughed at his own cleverness.

"It was a gift." I omitted mention of the giver's name.

He slipped it onto his wrist, next to the other bracelet.

"Thank you," he said. "I will enjoy this."

Supper was a constrained affair. All that night and during the next day the other boys cast troubled looks in his direction and mine. Marcus had made a few enemies already with his bullying, but his father was an aristocrat in good standing, and he, the family scion. I, on the other hand, was nobody. The fact that he was a known bully did not preclude my being a thief. I knew this thought must linger in some boys' minds as well. No doubt they all checked over their own possessions to be sure none of theirs went missing.

The following evening, we attended an official banquet at the palace, since Emperor Hadrian had returned to Rome.

Excited as always to see the emperor, I also felt heartsick that he might hear, if indeed he had not already, the story of the missing bracelet, and I hoped he proved as astute as I believed him to be in judging our two characters and ascertaining the truth of the situation.

Marcus already had arrived at the banquet hall, adorned with both bracelets and his expensive purple-striped toga, and settled on his couch for the evening by the time I got there. He spotted me standing just inside the doorway, trying to discover my own place assignment, since I wasn't serving that evening.

"Look, you're sitting by me, Antinous," he called out in a mock gesture of friendship. I had no choice but to go over to the couch where he already reclined and lie down alongside him.

Emperor Hadrian, after being officially seated at the head table next to the guest of honor, began to greet everyone at the nearby tables. When I saw how he noticed my bare arms I feared, and hoped. Then he spotted my copper bracelet glinting alongside the silver on Marcus' wrist. I saw his eyes narrow before turning my gaze to my plate.

"Marcus," Hadrian said, "where did you find that copper bracelet? It looks very much like one I just gave Antinous—and which, it seems, he has chosen not to wear this evening."

Hadrian looked at me then, one eyebrow lifted in query, and I gave him a pleading look in return while everyone else quieted down, waiting for Marcus to answer. Even the servants stood back and hushed, sensing a confrontation.

It gave me pleasure, I do admit, to watch how Marcus trembled, and stuttered his response, even as I dreaded the emperor's annoyance over our ridiculous schoolboy antics.

"Sir—it—it was a gift, Antinous gave me—"

"Sir," I said, interrupting my erstwhile accuser, "I

apologize. It is the same bracelet. I gave it to Marcus to make up for the loss of his silver one."

"But Marcus is wearing a silver bracelet," he said, pointing out the obvious in a wry voice. I felt certain then that the silver bracelet must not have been his gift to Marcus after all.

Relief infused me. I answered with more confidence.

"Yes, sir, but his had gone missing. Then, it turned up in my things somehow—"

Now Marcus interrupted me.

"It was a misunderstanding, sir, on my part," he said, slipping the copper bracelet from his wrist and handing it back to me. "I didn't realize—"

"I am quite sure, Marcus," the emperor said, in a dry tone, "that you did not."

Hadrian made a point of looking away just then, breaking eye contact with Marcus, to motion for more wine.

Korias, serving that night, passed by the couch where Marcus and I reclined, glanced at me and winked.

Marcus, glowing with humiliation, picked up his cup and drank without looking at anyone. I didn't dare look over at him.

Later I looked up to find Emperor Hadrian's amused eyes upon me. When I caught him, he smiled and gave me a little salute. That night was when I first noticed his hands, their particular beauty. (He is a man quite vain of his hands, which are shapely and almost hairless.)

I dropped my own eyes, allowed myself only a brief smile in return. It was wrong to gloat, and I sought to spare the wounded pride and mortified feelings of Marcus. I still needed to get along with him as best I could in school the next day, and the next.

At the end of that term, Marcus's father took his son off to their villa in the country for the greater part of the summer. When Marcus returned the next fall, he had grown taller and slimmer. In his behavior toward me, it seemed he had forgotten our quarrel. Still, I remained wary. Often, I caught him looking at me. Whenever I looked at him, he smiled.

SOON AFTER THE incident of the bracelets, I began to receive attention of another sort from a woman at court named Amyrra, the courtesan Hadrian favored at the time. She seemed to take a liking to me, and saw fit from time to time to whisper words of encouragement and instruction in my ear, as if I were a protégé of hers. I had to wonder why she took an interest in championing me—whether she was scheming to win a bet, or back a friend's, or best some rival of hers. She always made a point of talking to me at banquets and other gatherings. While she spoke, her hand brushed across my chest and then down, her touch light, a leaf falling alongside an oak trunk, a trick she employed to contrast her daintiness with the brawn of whatever male she addressed.

Pale as alabaster despite her claim of descent from ancient Nubian royalty, Amyrra outlined her eyes with kohl in the Egyptian style, which made them appear enormous. She always wore some subtle perfume, essence of jasmine mingled with another darker fragrance, intoxicating as wine. Expensive. As were her embroidered silken robes, her leather sandals, her many other adornments. Bracelets shimmered up and down both wrists while she gestured with graceful hands, hennaed palms turned out.

Rumor had it more than one patrician over the years vied for her company before she caught the emperor's eye, and she had managed all those attentions so as to retire a wealthy woman one day.

Once, after a performance of the tragedy *Hyacinthus*, Amyrra drew near while we were all drinking wine, and murmured her thoughts.

"Those men are considered great actors. Pah. We servants of love are the greatest actors of all." She tapped her fan on my forearm.

"Oh, now, Antinous, don't look shocked. Surely you don't think you've been brought all the way to Rome just to serve wine and join the civil service someday. Believe me, acting is our true calling—along with a bit of thievery. With our sighs, our glances, the subtleties of lips and limbs, we must steal the affections of our targets. We must be as nimble as the pickpockets in the forum who thrive on purloined gleanings."

I laughed at that, although her assumptions about my position at court offended me. Assumptions that, of course, were later proved right.

"It's true," she said. "Think about it, darling. How I envy those fellow thieves of ours. After all, they get to practice first on their straw dummies tied with bells. We must succeed at once, or fail. Men are fickle—though they can be made to shake like a sistrum. We must never forget to give thanks to Mercury, god of messengers, physicians, and thieves."

She laughed then, and went gliding off to visit with a different guest.

Another evening, during a banquet that stretched on for hours, she flitted to my cushion, studied my face for a moment, and said, "It seems you've already made quite an impression on our emperor, my dear."

While I fumbled for a reply, she said, "That's wonderful. Of course, Hadrian isn't one to be captured by a pretty face alone. He's a man whose mind must be captivated as well.

"I hear you're a bright lad, not just a handsome one. So apply yourself, Antinous, to Latin as well as protocol, and get past this annoying bashfulness of yours. Don't be ashamed of your background—to a jaded palate, simple fare can be refreshing.

"Yes," she said, touching just the fingertips of her right hand to my chin and turning my face this way and that, "I do believe you have real potential."

"Potential for what, please?"

"Why, what else?" she said, and gave me a teasing smile. "To become the new favorite, of course. But believe me, with all the choices available, that's no easy task. Take care, Antinous, and study. That's all I'll say for now."

She slipped away then, bracelets twinkling, on the hunt for someone else to beguile.

Later, I mulled her words, wondering if they were true. It was understood in court who the emperor's current favorite was then—Lucius Commodus, the young patrician of the court, several years older than I, of whom Hadrian seemed quite fond.

Commodus never spoke to me, as if I were the servant of someone he didn't know. I understood why Amyrra thought he might be put aside soon. Handsome, cultured, rich, and charming though he was, he could no longer be called a boy. Commodus was soon taking on the white toga of manhood, and so now must officially be considered a Roman citizen, a man—and thus, too old to continue to be the emperor's consort, his eromenos, beloved youth.

WHAT A HAPPY hound I was in those green and gold days, content to bask beneath the emperor's gaze, loll at his feet and watch him in silence. Looking back, I can see how such adoration, innocent though it was, might well seduce its object with as much efficacy as the oft-honed skills of a jade.

I listened, fascinated, whenever Hadrian spoke of battles he had fought in and sights he had encountered. I was enchanted by his evocation of the lands of snow, of barbarians whose skill with horses surpassed any Roman's, as if a new race of centaurs had emerged upon the earth. He described the symbols adorning their crude battle equipment, spirals turning and returning, representing an idea of infinity.

He told of how one Celtic chieftain, a woman, captured in battle while fighting alongside the men of her tribe (for the barbarians hold that women rule with as much wisdom as men), waited for the moment when her hands were released from the manacles, seized a dagger from the belt of one of the soldiers guarding her, and plunged it into her own chest. Though a woman, she held death preferable to the dishonor awaiting her in Rome.

In those days I clung to his every pronouncement as if he were Socrates and I Plato, gathering jewels of wisdom to hand on to some Aristotle of the future. In my youthful arrogance, I believed that because Hadrian revered Greek culture, he thought that I, being Greek, was superior to my fellows. Only much later did it occur to me that he, being emperor, bestowed superiority upon me because he fancied my being Greek.

Then one night, as Korias and I stood stacking empty wine jugs in a corner after a banquet for the kitchen workers to retrieve later, one of the guards sought me out.

"The emperor wishes to see you," he said.

I returned to the banquet room, where Hadrian still sat at his table. He smiled and waved me closer. I knelt beside the couch where he reclined with his trusted prefect, Marcius Turbo. When he leaned over to speak to me, I caught the scent of the oil he wore in his hair, a citrus fragrance.

"I remember telling you, Antinous, about a hunting lodge I have near the Arcadian woods. The stable master assures me that you can ride, and the hunt master says you can aim a deadly spear. You also seem to enjoy the company of horses and hounds. So you will attend me as groom on our next boar hunt, about a month from now."

I felt myself blush with excitement, and knew the red must be blooming in both cheeks. (Feelings have always betrayed me in blood this way.)

"I'm honored, sir," I said. He smiled again, enjoying my pleasure and confusion.

"Speak with the stable master, then, and he'll give my permission to the school master for you to miss a few days. I trust you'll have no trouble getting caught up once we return."

"Thank you, sir," I said. "No, sir, in most subjects I've read a little ahead."

"I suspected as much," he said. "Thank you, Antinous. That's all for now."

I departed with as much grace as I could muster, once I stopped gawking at him like an addled fawn.

"WHAT IS IT, Antinous?" Korias asked, curiosity overcoming his usual restraint. He and a few other pages lingered in the dusty road just outside the palace wall, eager to find out why I had been summoned.

"The Emperor wants me to serve as his groom," I said, and felt the hairs stand up along my forearms, from both the chill of the night air and the excitement of speaking those words aloud.

"That's quite an honor," Korias said, looking at me as if seeing me anew. "Congratulations."

"Yes," I said. "I believe the stable master told him I'd be good company for the hounds."

Korias and the others laughed, which reassured me. I didn't want to sound either too arrogant or too eager in revealing this new assignment from Hadrian.

As if he realized my awkwardness at that moment, Korias changed the subject to the evening's musical selections. I gave him a grateful look for his tact while he criticized a lyre player for her inferior technique.

Still, the other boys whispered and snickered, and a couple cast glances naked with envy when we made our way by torchlight back to our quarters.

At the next banquet, serving wine alongside Korias, I felt his eyes on me while we lounged against the wall between rounds.

"You know, Antinous," he said, "you've cut quite a figure at court already—and now, with this invitation from the emperor himself, you must be careful. The knives will be bared, so to speak, in certain quarters."

Hearing this, I sighed and touched my old childhood amulet from my grandparents, which I still wore beneath my new linen tunic, for protection.

"I know you're right," I said. "Marcus seems to hate me, and this will only add fuel to the brazier."

"To be honest, I was thinking more of Commodus," said Korias. He scanned the banquet room as if to make sure no one noticed us conversing.

"For all his charm, he's as two-faced as Janus. Don't be taken in. He's long been considered the emperor's favorite, and he won't relish Hadrian's attention to anyone else—especially since he took the white toga. He probably feels less sure of Hadrian now, since they can no longer sleep together. Officially, anyhow."

I decided to trust Korias.

"You know Amyrra?"

"The courtesan, yes," he said.

"She told me, she thinks—forgive me, this must sound so arrogant—she thinks I might become a new favorite. She's been encouraging me, even offering little hints and suggestions here and there. I can't help but wonder why."

Korias lifted one eyebrow and grinned, his white teeth flashing.

"Oh, I can tell you why," he said. "She's a good one to have as an ally. Here, let's make our rounds again, and then let me tell you a story."

We hurried to serve the guests, pouring out the next round of watered wine with as much haste as possible without sloshing it on anyone, then refilled the flagons of wine and water from the kitchen reserves so that we could resume our positions along the wall.

Speaking in a low voice to avoid being overheard, Korias inclined toward me and continued.

"When I was a first-year myself, I heard from an older friend of mine that Amyrra hates Commodus—though of course she must tread carefully there, since he is a patrician, and a favorite of Hadrian's besides."

I felt a stab of jealousy, wondering just who this older friend had been.

"But why," I said, forcing myself to refocus on the conversation. "How did Commodus offend her?"

"Well, it seems," Korias said, "that during a banquet his father sponsored, Commodus thought they needed more wine, so he asked Amyrra to send her man down to the shops for a few more flasks—quite a few more.

"Of course, she did so at once, not wanting to offend a friend of Hadrian's, and thinking she might even forge a helpful alliance with this favor.

"But then, after having her put all of that wine on her own credit, Commodus never did get around to having his father reimburse her. Despite all his wealth—or maybe because of it—he has a talent for spending other people's money."

Korias gave me another little grin. He skimmed one fingertip across the wine in the mouth of the amphora beside him to fish out a couple of midges that had bumbled their way into the jar and now floated on the dark sea of wine. He shook his finger. The live one flew off. The other clung to his fingertip, drowned already, so he flicked it away with a surreptitious motion and wiped his finger against the gold hem of his tunic.

"How unfair," I said, "to take advantage of her that way."

"Yes," Korias said, "and Amyrra has never forgotten or forgiven him for it."

"I can imagine," I said. "That may explain her interest in me—or rather, in the emperor's supposed interest in me."

"Well, partly," he said, "but like everyone else here in court, she has an eye for beauty."

The blood beat at my temples. Korias, always so proper and focused on duty, was flirting with me. I cast him a sideways glance, one like Amyrra practiced on me.

"What a kind thing to say."

Now it appeared to be his turn to blush. "It's just the truth. You're very attractive."

I let myself relax and slide over toward him, feeling his shoulder and arm tense in anticipation as I moved against him.

"You're very attractive yourself, Korias."

My compliment was rewarded with an audible intake of breath on his part, a tremor that seemed to pulse between his body and mine.

And after the banquet, by means of various dissemblings, the two of us somehow managed to find ourselves alone on a mild and moonlit night.

Out of sight of the palace wall, we melted together into the shade of an oak, kisses interrupted by murmurs leading to more kisses. Never again could I smell the green reassurance of oak leaves without thinking of Korias and that night.

Pressing against his body with the full length of mine, I felt our mutual excitement wrestling together and, crouching a little, shifted myself to one side in a gesture of accommodation. Grazing the warm hollow of his throat with my mouth, I let my fingers stroke along that cloaked throbbing below, so like my own, and he moaned.

But when I reached for the hem of his tunic, anxious to grasp that lovely column hidden behind a facade of linen, hoping he would reciprocate, he groaned and stayed my hand.

"No, Antinous," he said, pulling away, albeit with evident reluctance, "we can't. It wouldn't be right."

My own frustration grew as my excitement ebbed.

"No," Korias said, his voice firm. "It wouldn't be—honorable."

I understood his intentions, which were noble. He believed the emperor might be interested in me; therefore he must not poach the emperor's quarry. But I wanted that other firmness, offered and then withdrawn.

Back in my quarters, unable to sleep, with my own hand I found myself again and again in the dark. Imagining first Korias, then Hadrian, I thought I might faint from love.

IN THE WEEKS leading up to the boar hunt, Momius, the stable master, familiarized me with a few imperial protocols to be observed at the hunting lodge, suggesting which horses should be assigned to which riders, and which might need relieving after a day—both horses and riders. He told me to reserve Xanthus and Balius, fastest and strongest, for Hadrian and the hunt master. I was to ride an older horse, Pelas.

One thing Momius didn't specify was where I might be quartered on the trip. I assumed that, as a groom, I would stay in a small shelter of some sort near the dogs and horses. Upon reaching the lodge, however, I learned otherwise.

We arrived late, having stopped for a meal along the way. Along with the other grooms I helped feed, water and brush the horses, checking their hooves for signs of cracking or other damage, and afterward fed the hounds. Then, kit in hand, I looked around in the bunk room trying to decide where I might be most comfortable for the night. I had just knelt down to take off my sandals and wash my feet when one of the others spoke.

"Antinous, Hadrian will expect you to stay in his quarters, since you are his personal attendant."

He looked at me with an ambiguous expression, one I had difficulty deciphering in the twilight.

"Oh, I didn't realize. Thank you," I said. "Good night, then."

I slipped my sandals back onto my clean feet, picked up my bundle and walked to the main lodge, and nervous excitement caused my breath and pulse to quicken as if I had run up a steep hill. Inside, I followed the house servant to Hadrian's private quarters.

I was ushered into his presence where he sat at a small desk with his scribe, Phlegon, beside him. At that time, I didn't realize Phlegon was an author in his own right, undertaking to write a history of the Olympic games. Later, I heard him read from his *Book of Marvels* while we were at court in Athens.

Both men greeted me, and Hadrian invited me to sit on the couch. He chatted with me in a desultory manner for several minutes while they finished some correspondence. I watched him use his signet ring to imbed his mark in the sealing wax of several scrolls, just as he once sealed his invitation to me.

Hadrian wore a simple, expensive robe, beneath which the muscles of his chest gleamed in the lamplight whenever he turned to speak to me. I felt shy, and cannot remember now either that of which he spoke or my own responses, which were no doubt inane. I didn't know what to do with my own hands. As soon as he finished dictating his last missive, Phlegon departed, leaving the stylus and other apparatus of his trade behind on the desk.

Hadrian rose from his chair and came over to me—I stood again, when he did—and put his palms against both sides of my face. For a moment he stood motionless, staring into my eyes.

"So beautiful," he said, and my own image swam before me in his pupils, dark as night.

His face just then amazed me. Not his gaze, not a smile or any expression crossing his features. Rather, the apparition of his face at that moment, a sun breaking from behind a pillow of cloud, radiance lighting upon him, upon us both.

Then he did an odd thing. He placed his hands upon both of my shoulders, a mute insistence.

I understood that I must kneel, go down on one knee before him. My head inclined in a bow, a loyal subject paying tribute to his ruler. The ancient words of Aeschylus describing the Greeks, which we had just read in school a few days earlier, hummed like bees of reproach in my ears: "They bow to no man, and are no man's slaves."

When I tried to rise again, his hands resisted. His robe, unbound, fell open in front of me.

After a moment, I realized what he wanted. I felt shame and anger, which I struggled to douse. This act I knew of, and certainly had heard about at school. I had seen the paintings at the baths. It was what one sometimes engaged in with a prostitute, or perhaps a servant or younger classmate. I was no slave, no girl, and this act I expected, anticipated, being done only to me, for me. By the Roman code, I knew, such submission was not asked of a partner, for it demeaned him.

But perhaps he meant to follow ancient Greek custom, intended to take a youth as his lover, to train him in the duties and responsibilities of citizenship, and then release him upon the arrival of his own manhood. Such submission to an older lover was still allowed with no dishonor until one came of age. I gave him my compliance.

Afterward I spit him out into my hand cloth with all the discretion I could muster. It smelled just like my own. I had always thought of sex as a red fish darting, an image gleaned from some erotic Egyptian poem, no doubt. Naïve boy, I expected silver or gold splashes, somehow, but he possessed the same flesh, the same seed, as any man.

THE NEXT MORNING, as if in a trance, I helped the hunt master and the other grooms ready the dogs and horses to ride out, and looked around at the great forest that engulfed us, dwarfing the lodge. These trees were the robust pines and firs of my childhood, not those parasols which consort with cypress all over Italy. That familiar wood, dappled with sunlight, comforted me, dazed as I was by my abrupt transition from boy to consort.

The next night I learned what else he wanted from me. It hurt.

Stoic, I said nothing, and did not cry out, so that Priapus, sating his lust, indulged in a private orgy to rival Messalina's. On the hillsides of my childhood I had watched bulls and heifers, rams and ewes, randy goats going at one another, heard the older boys snicker about sheep and shepherds. But I never imagined myself as the mounted one.

The morning sun saw my blood on the bedclothes, despite Hadrian's lavish use of warm, scented oil. When he went outside to relieve himself, I stripped away the stained sheet, replacing it with a fresh one. If he noticed, he said nothing.

THAT NEXT AFTERNOON, Hadrian once again proved to all his prowess when he tracked down an enormous black boar and dispatched it with one thrust of his spear, driving it into the heart of the pig until he buried it up to the shaft. His mount still quivered and gasped for air after the pursuit, sides heaving in and out like bellows. Everyone kept up the shouting and rejoicing (I perhaps the loudest) while he claimed his trophy with delibera-tion and then pulled the hem of his hunting cloak over his head to silence us before he offered up the first meats of his quarry as a lustration for the success of the hunt.

Riding Pelas all day left my hindquarters in agony, a burning pain I took care to keep to myself. I suppose the thought never occurred to Hadrian that horseback might be a torment for me after the previous night's activities. That evening I sat in a cool bath for as long as I dared before anyone began looking for me.

The scent of evergreens enveloping those Arcadian morn-ings acted as tonic for Hadrian. His brow smoothed itself, released from the usual furrows of worry, and a sweeter side began to emerge from behind his brusque manner.

Responding to the fresh air and beauty of our surroundings, my own maturing, recovered body also reacted as one might expect. I woke every morning with an erection, and to my surprise he often expected me to make use of this.

During those early bouts of lovemaking, my fear and shyness abating, I studied his naked body, which held the story of his life in its contours, ridges and protuberances. Old scars, calluses, and healed breaks at collarbone and rib bore witness to his youthful military career and hunting expeditions. An ugly gash seamed through his thigh, carved by the tusk of a boar, one of few creatures which ever managed to wound him. Tanned, muscular, his body betrayed his age only with a bit of slackening at the belly; a certain softness beneath his upper arms.

It seemed a privilege to be one of those few, besides his bath attendants, who ever saw the emperor in such a state of nature. But the first time that he, in turn, knelt before me, horror threaded the sensation—as if I were watching a noble fir bent to the ground by the passing of Dionysos, succumbing to a tumult of uncontrollable force. I closed my eyes and clenched my hands at my sides, not daring to tangle them in the hair of the emperor. Nor did I allow my hips to push forward against the source of that pleasure, though they ached to do so.

Afterward, I waited until I knew he had risen, put on his robe and turned away from me before I opened my eyes. It seemed the only way to conduct myself with the proper show of respect. He had spit my seed onto the floor. I mopped it up with one of my hand cloths.

In the mornings I prepared his simple breakfast—melons ripe and glistening, bread fresh-baked and fragrant, with such white, utter loveliness hidden within its brown crust. The pleasure of the knife, slicing, astonished me.

On one such morning, waking before my companion, I rose on one elbow and studied Hadrian's face in repose. Asleep, he looked different, his features robbed of their normal expression. Then his eyes opened.

"Don't," he said.

"What?"

"Don't look at me when I'm sleeping."

"Why not?"

"Because I am not myself then."

"All right," I said, "then you must promise never to look upon me, either, when I sleep."

He laughed and sat up on his elbow to look into my face.

"You're wise," he said. "Sleep is a most indifferent lover, like his brother Death, and cares not who reposes in his arms, a seducer with no regard for individuals, and no favorites."

He took me in his own arms then, the conversation ended.

HADRIAN SOON ACKNOWLEDGED our new intimacy in public by causing several new projects to be undertaken in Arcadia, including a new temple for Neptune, and the restoration of the tomb of Epaminondas and his companion. He also offered a she-bear skin to Eros at the spring of Narcissus. The pelt, removed from the animal that bore it, having undergone all manner of treatment meant to cure it, nonetheless remained impregnated with a stench of carrion—a fine metaphor for love, I now see.

After our return to Rome, at the banquet to welcome Hadrian back to court, Amyrra came up and kissed me on the cheek and said, "I knew it. You've become lovers. I can tell—Hadrian looks giddy and moon-fed."

Her pleasure found an echo, somewhat less smug, on certain faces around us during the meal. Others there seemed either oblivious or else displeased by Hadrian's signaling of a new relationship with me. Commodus behaved with indifference toward me and even toward Hadrian that evening, behavior intended to cut as much as possible without showing contempt to the emperor.

I began to accompany Hadrian at all times as the acknowledged new favorite, trotting at his side like a dog or a wife—just like the one who would be chosen and fobbed onto me someday at the appropriate moment; that time when the clouds obscure the sun, as the saying goes; when I, like Commodus, grow too old to remain the beloved.

I wanted to give Hadrian a gift in return after all his displays of affection, but nothing seemed appropriate. At last I decided to give him a set of cloths like my own, which I always found useful. At the market, I found a soft Egyptian cotton, pure white. When the seamstress stitched them up for me, I asked her also to embroider his signet in one corner of each with gold thread. I found the effect charming, and when I presented the set to Hadrian, he seemed pleased.

Yet for several weeks, well after our return to the city, nightmares disrupted my sleep, Cyclops, giants, various monsters always pursuing me until I woke.

In the mornings, I rose with the dawn in order to slip from his bedchamber before his barber and other attendants arrived, and made my way back to my own quarters while the aromas from bakery ovens filled the streets and birds rose like prayers from nests beneath the eaves of apartment buildings. This remained my routine until the next trip into the country with Hadrian. When we returned to Rome afterward, I was presented with my own bedchamber adjacent to his, and found all my belongings from school already in residence there.

Back in my classes again, it pleased me, vain little peacock, to note how several of the other boys, including Marcus, had taken to carrying small hand cloths, in imitation of Hadrian, and of me. Korias had chosen a subtle grey, while Marcus favored scarlet. Even at court, some men began to carry them after Hadrian made a point of flourishing one during a banquet. That acknowledgement delighted me. He didn't intend to start a fashion—yet one began.

Commodus did not take up the trend. Instead, he played a trick on me, toward the end of one night's banquet, to show just where I, a wine bearer, stood with him. He called my name in a soft voice and held out a linen dinner napkin, emblazoned with the imperial crest, folded like a sack around some hidden contents. As I took it, he gave me a dazzling smile and walked out of the banquet room.

The napkin was full of bones, remnants of the quail he had eaten at supper. I was glad he didn't bother to stop and watch me open his nasty surprise. In his absence, he could not see me blush with anger; nor could I speak words in haste that I might regret later. Instead, I

77

chose to ignore this insult, just as he always ignored me. Whenever I saw him afterward, I made sure to behave with neither more nor less courtesy than before.

About this time, Hadrian began to present me with frequent tokens of affection—books, incense, a silver mirror—which, I believe, were meant to signify a certain ascendance of my position at court. His enjoyment of my companionship seemed genuine. He appreciated my habit of maintaining silence in his presence, which allowed him to think, or work, or rest as he chose.

Sometimes when we sat alone together, he recited poems he had composed, or sang, or played a melancholy air upon the flute. That was an instrument I always avoided for fear that playing it made my face appear ugly and ridiculous. (I deferred to the wisdom of Athena, who, disgusted by her reflection in a river while playing, once tossed her own flute away.) But I did often accompany him upon the lyre, which I might play with proper decorum. I also recited the verses of Sappho, though I never recited for him my own cento based on her work. I admired the tenth muse, but also recognized that I myself was not one.

Hadrian once confessed to me his youthful nickname, the Greekling, with its veiled insults implying effeminacy and treachery, after I told him how the Roman boys teased me, referring to me as young Ulysses. Romans consider our Greek Odysseus too sly in his reliance on wit, rather than strength and courage. Yet it was he who thought up the horse which broke the Trojans.

PLOTINA, THE WIDOWED empress of Trajan and Hadrian's adoptive mother, now took an interest in me. This woman, Hadrian's greatest political ally and mentor, had arranged for his marriage to Trajan's great-niece, Sabina, in order to cement his alliance with her husband. The union proved a political success, if not a fruitful one, and assured Hadrian's succession to the throne upon her husband's demise. Plotina's ambitions for Hadrian were exceeded only perhaps by his own; she believed him capable of greatness.

I came upon her as if by accident one afternoon in the palace gardens, where she sat on a marble bench beside a shrine graced with a statue of the goddess Aphrodite and her companion nymphs. A fountain burbled behind them. Topiary shrubs spiraled around the flagstones of the path, and from pear trees nearby came the chirruping of birds kept in one of the aviaries.

"Good afternoon," she said, acting as if she were surprised to discover me there as well. "A lovely day, isn't it?"

Plotina must have gleaned from some of the servants that I often walked there when I had a few moments of free time. I wondered how long it took her to pick her way to that bench through the droppings from the free-roaming flock of peacocks. She had taken care that their ubiquitous excrement should not soil her dainty sandals.

Like Lucretia reborn, Plotina always appeared to embody purity, as befits an aristocratic Roman matron. Despite knowing, from a comment Hadrian once made, that her elaborate hairstyle alone required an hour of dressing by her attendants each morning, I do not believe she was a vain woman at all. Her coiffure, like the heavy gold jewels and tasteful, expensive clothing she wore, merely announced her status, confirmed her position in society—wife to one emperor, foster to another. That

elaborate styling became as much a component of a desig-
nated uniform as the crested helmet worn by a centurion.

I greeted her with deference, and she asked me to be
seated. After we chatted for a few moments, she began,
with her customary diplomacy, to sound me out about
the depth and dimensions of my fledgling relationship
with her foster son.

Soon satisfied, or so it appeared, by my answers, and
deeming her task accomplished, she took her leave of me
with a paean of praise for Hadrian and a proffering of
advice to me.

"Be kind to him, Antinous," she said, looking deep
into my eyes. "Like Atlas, he bears the world upon those
shoulders."

Her stern gaze softened as she spoke.

"Be sweet and loving, and listen to him, without judging or competing. Let others try to impress him by showing off. In time, a successor will be found from among
the aristocracy, someone like Lucius Commodus, or even
Hadrian's own nephew, Pedanius Fuscus. What he needs
right now, above all, is someone who is appreciative, all-
accepting—someone who will love him just as he is."

I took those words to heart, gratified by her faith in
my ability to love Hadrian as he needed to be loved. In
those halcyon days, I still saw in him my Zeus, Apollo,
Odysseus bearing his boar-tusk scar. I fancied myself his
Ganymede, Hyacinthus, Penelope. I worshipped him like
a Christian, flesh and blood upon my tongue. Plotina
divined this, of course, as if it were inscribed upon my
pink and guileless face.

"You see Jupiter in him, don't you?" she asked. "And
yourself, the cupbearer." Her voice was light, almost

girlish, but her eyes held mine in steady regard. I could not tell whether she mocked me.

Plotina remained concerned above all with Hadrian's well-being—he whom she had supported, abetted, even, some whispered, lied and forged for, to assure his succession to the throne. Others whispered that they were lovers, but I never saw in the rectitude of their behavior any indication of such an adulterous relationship. In all of their dealings, her attitude seemed that of a proud, watchful mother; his, that of a respectful son seeking out her wisdom.

I realize now that all the various kindnesses shown to me by Plotina at court were truly meant for Hadrian. While she bore me no ill will, nor malice or jealousy, neither did she give a single fig regarding my own interests, needs, or well-being. I was a subject she deemed beyond reproach, a love interest of whom she approved.

OVER TIME, I also began to perceive the subtle ways in which my lover was attempting to break me, just as he might gentle a horse or dog, to gain obedience while maintaining trust. Hadrian tested me all the time, demanding my acquiescence through various acts of control and manipulation—acquiescence I would have given of my own accord if only I had been allowed.

Once, I recall, while I sat watching him work at the correspondence desk in his private quarters, he held up a ring sent by yet another supplicant, a blue stone mounted in a four-pronged setting of silver.

"Do you know what stone this is?" he asked me, turning it this way and that in the lamplight.

"Lapis," I said, pleased to be able to respond at once, mistaken in my thought that he too would be pleased, proud of my knowledge.

He was not.

As I discovered when I stood and went over to him thinking to claim a kiss, a prize he denied by turning his head away to one side, sullen as a child. That gesture of pettiness both amused and cut me to my core. I had not realized the question as posed meant a win-lose game, nor that he expected me to forfeit if I knew the answer. At least Phlegon, gone off to fetch more ink, didn't witness the ugliness of that little scene.

Sensing my hurt and disappointment in him, Hadrian relented and dropped a swift, begrudging kiss onto the side of my neck just below my jaw—more to save face, I think, than to reassure me. I never saw that particular ring again, nor did I ask what became of it.

At the first festival of Jupiter I attended as his acknowledged beloved, Hadrian humiliated Korias and embarrassed me during the horse race. We all sat on the imperial dais overlooking the Sacred Way, and when the horses came rushing along the street, Korias looked over at me and smiled. Hadrian must have thought he held my gaze a little too long, because he leaned in from the other side of me and said, "The horses just went that way, gentlemen."

Korias, stricken, swiveled to look in the other direction, where the horses soon approached the finish line at the foot of the Capitoline. I, too, turned to watch them, feeling Hadrian's gaze burn into my neck. His hand pressed against the folds of purple-striped toga at the small of my back, but I refused to lean against it in acknowledgement of that gesture of intimacy.

After the race ended, as soon as the winning mount had been offered up to Jupiter and its head removed for the priests while the smell of charred horseflesh wafted up into the hills, Korias gave a courteous nod to Hadrian and to me, not meeting our eyes, and hurried from the platform, his purple-striped toga swirling about him, to lose himself in the crowd and recover his equanimity. I ached for him. I knew he felt mortified.

"Why did you—" I started to ask, but stopped. One does not question the emperor.

Hadrian smiled at me, at his ease. He may have assumed I felt flattered, pleased by his possessiveness. Had it been some other boy—say, Marcus—who caught that lash, my vanity well might have plumped like a toadstool. But not when it landed on Korias. Not him.

"A nice boy," Hadrian said. "A little sensitive, perhaps. I didn't mean anything, of course—just a bit of good-natured teasing."

"Of course."

Knowing Korias as I did, I knew he was the last person Hadrian ever need warn away from my affections. Korias' own sense of honor precluded any such necessity.

Hadrian's behavior that afternoon also struck me as somewhat hypocritical, since even I had heard the gossip about Hadrian's own earlier days at court, before he became emperor. While Trajan still reigned, the story alleged, he and Hadrian almost feuded over a couple of boys serving in the page corps. Only a warning from a mutual friend, no doubt instigated at Plotina's discretion, intervened and kept Hadrian from an assignation with one of them—the one for which

Trajan might never have forgiven him. Hadrian turned for solace to a couple of senators' wives instead. So the gossip avowed, anyway.

HADRIAN MUST NOT have been much loved as a child, I think, to so mistrust love as an adult that he prefers being in control to being in love. Even so, from time to time, I looked up to catch his face unguarded, and found it just then swamped with love, as my own also must have looked, at least early on—at times it seemed to me that we circled like combatants in the ring, always dancing around and away from that small, red-hot, unspeakable word. Reeking with all the old fear of the cave, death. Our gods, ancestors, surely still smell it on us.

When Socrates and Phaedrus discussed love beneath a plane tree, the former described how love can transform, the latter, how it can deform. Hadrian's love has deformed me, because both his nature and his office demand he must always, always win. This in turn demands that I must always, always lose to him.

Not enough for Hadrian to have the upper hand—he must raze the field, break the spine, crack open the opponent and devour his entrails. Yet his arrogance masks depths of insecurity, and fear of emotion, whether his own or anyone else's.

He has always surrounded himself, when in Rome and traveling as well, with the most brilliant minds of our day—Apollodorus, Juvenal, Tacitus, Seutonius, Plutarch, Arrian, Marcellus, Favorinus, and many others—yet always he feels compelled to best them in their own area of expertise, and woe to any man who refuses to yield to his opinion. Hadrian is far more open and kind in engagements with any common man of the street than in discourses with these men—no doubt because the former poses no threat to him, or rather his sense of superiority.

Such revelations of Hadrian's character over time, while increasing my understanding, also acted as slow poison on my respect and affection for the man.

How pure his love for horses and hounds, though, his admiration of their grace and courage in the face of boar, bear, lion. He once built a monument for his favorite horse, Borysthenes, after its death, in the manner of Alexander, who honored his own racer, Bucephalus, in similar fashion, even naming a city after him.

Hadrian rides as if he and the horse were one; he once took down a boar with one blow; yet the killing is not, I think, what he revels in, but rather that state, almost of time suspended, one enters into with animals in nature—those which are hunted, and those which partake of the hunt.

An expert marksman, he claims to be impressed by my own ability to use either hand for a throw or thrust. I tried to eat with my left hand when I was small, but my father and grandfather discouraged this flaw, adamant in teaching me that one's left must bear up the shield, leaving one's right free to strike. Training the right arm to do the work to which the left seems inclined makes either arm sufficient, if necessity demands.

Hadrian also holds to a Platonic ideal for breeding his favorite creatures. By establishing standards for each breed, to which animals must conform before being allowed to mate, the most desirable characteristics and abilities can be preserved. Dogs bred in this way to herd livestock often can be seen, while yet in clumsy puppyhood, circling close to the sheep in the fields and dropping to a crouch, trying to corral the flock by instinct before their masters have even begun training them.

Hadrian never has shared my fascination with cats, those hunters sacred to the Egyptians, bred and revered for their regal beauty, symbols of the great goddess. Feline instincts betray too much cruelty, I suppose, to win his admiration. They enjoy tormenting prey, whereas Hadrian prefers to believe his own cruelties are not innate but practical, methodical, means to achieve his ends—and allay his fears.

I have always suspected that Hadrian's travels to the far reaches of the empire not only give him a clear picture of the holdings over which he rules, but also provide an excuse not to attend the spectacles in the Flavian amphitheatre any more often than required in his official capacity as ruler. Such orgies of blood do not represent to him, a Spaniard by origin and temperament, the truth of the hunt, in which each kill is hallowed for the hunter by a spirit of engagement with the beast of prey.

While he enjoys the chariot races held in the Circus Maximus, favoring the Green teams over the Red, White and Blue, and always attends the race for the October Horse during the Jupiter festivities, I believe the killing of human beings in the ring for sport appalls him far more than he can prudently reveal. With regard to duties and privileges alike, the emperor must remain, or appear to remain, disinterested in order to best fulfill his office. In this way, the most powerful often becomes a servant to the desires of those over whom he rules.

These past few years, I have accompanied Hadrian on his travels and with him have seen much of this sprawl of empire, every corner of which he is determined to visit. A poet he considers a friend, Florus, once wrote a poem to tease him about his peripatetic habits:

"I don't want to be a Caesar
Plodding around Britain
Freezing my nuts off
in a Scythian midden."

Hadrian knew Florus' poem was a tribute, disguised, yet as always he couldn't resist trying to top it:

"I don't want to be a Florus
Crawling around pubs,
Skulking in pie-shops
Bitten by bugs."

On my first visit to Athens with Hadrian, I had my first glimpse of the Acropolis, with the Parthenon gleaming atop the city like a crown scoured pure by the Greek sun. I thought of Pythagoras, Plato, the dream of harmony in a perfect city, music of the spheres. It remains the only sight from my travels which overwhelmed me to the point of tears.

In Athens also I made the acquaintance of Favorinus of Arles, the notorious Gaul, hermaphrodite, nemesis of Polemo, and gadfly of a philosopher. He was one of the few men besides the philosopher Secundus and the architect Apollodorus brave enough, or foolhardy enough, to contradict Hadrian to his face. He likes to boast of himself, "I am a eunuch tried for adultery, a barbarian who speaks Greek, and one who has quarreled with the emperor, yet remains alive."

The first time I saw Favorinus, draped in a fuchsia cloak shot with gold thread, I thought, what an ugly woman. But when we drew nearer and the beardless mouth opened, I realized the lapidary voice that issued forth belonged to no woman.

Two-sexed as Tiresias, without the seer's accompanying blindness, Favorinus is a lotus forged of iron, slippery as a barrel of eels, gaudy as a kingdom of parrots, audacious as the raven which hailed Tiberius as Caesar, thus earning its own burial procession in Rome (if Pliny is to be believed).

Favorinus told me how his fierce Gaulish mother loved her child without reservation. She once told her husband that if he cut off the baby's appurtenance, as he sometimes threatened, she would not hesitate to cut off his. Her acceptance allowed Favorinus to gird those dual loins with confidence, even exuberance, or so I believe.

On our first encounter there in Athens, Favorinus greeted me with a funny little speech, tossed off impromptu, or so we were meant to think:

"Welcome, Antinous, star of the east, fresh from Nikomedia, successor of Caesar as Queen of Bithynia, engaging new favorite now engaging our favorite emperor." Embracing me, he said in a stage whisper calculated to amuse all bystanders in the palace courtyard, "And how is your bum, darling—still sore from all that riding, hmm."

For my ears alone, he added, "Allow me to recommend a paste of comfrey root powder and olive oil. Quite soothing. Do try it."

I soon realized that despite his flamboyance, or perhaps because of it, Favorinus commanded respect from many quarters, although he also had his detractors. Among them were a consul who charged him with adultery (and whom he did indeed appear to have cuckolded), as well as his longstanding rival in rhetoric, Polemo.

It was Favorinus who told me the story of Hadrian's confrontation with the philosopher Secundus on a long-ago trip Hadrian made to Athens.

Secundus had taken a vow of silence in remorse over his mother's suicide, since she killed herself after failing a test of chastity he set before her. Hadrian tested the philosopher's vow, trying to command him to speak—even on pain of death. Secundus refused to yield. Seeing this, Hadrian then set Secundus to answer twenty questions, in writing, regarding the nature of the universe. The philosopher's written responses mocked and prodded the emperor's own fears and pretensions. Favorinus recited his favorite of Secundus' responses to Hadrian for me:

"Boast not that you alone have encircled the world in your travels, for it is only the sun and the moon and the stars that really make the journey around it. Moreover, do not think of yourself as being beautiful and great and rich and the ruler of the inhabited world. Know you not that, being a man, you were born to be Life's plaything, helpless in the hands of Fortune and Destiny, sometimes exalted, sometimes humbled lower than the grave?"

Even Favorinus was not as bold as Secundus, for he once conceded a public argument with the emperor over some minor point of grammar. Though Favorinus was correct, as he later liked to say, "I felt I must concede, for I do not have thirty legions at my own disposal."

During my first visit to the court of Athens with Hadrian then, Favorinus persuaded Phlegon to entertain us by reading passages from his work in progress,

Book of Marvels, a compendium of odd phenomena such as the discovery of live centaurs (one of which was embalmed by the prefect of Egypt and sent to Rome during Augustus' rule), a baby with the head of Anubis, a two-headed baby (the high priests recommended it be cast into the Tiber), and reports of males giving birth.

In this work Phlegon also had compiled a list of various individuals reported to have undergone spontaneous sex changes, most often young girls of marriageable age who suddenly extruded male genitals, although the legendary Teiresias changed from male to female and back again after an encounter with Apollo, then was blinded and accorded the gift of augury in a fateful encounter with Zeus and Hera, the account of which amused Favorinus in particular. The passage of Phlegon's book which I found most fascinating recounted prophecies recorded in the ancient book of Sibylline oracles and never before revealed in public, or so he claimed.

Later, at Eleusis, Hadrian and I both received initiations into the mysteries of Demeter and Persephone—I as a novitiate, he into a higher echelon of grace—over three days and three nights of revelation honoring the sacred cycles of transformation, of which one may not speak in keeping with the solemn vow of devotion.

Once, while visiting Crete, we saw paintings of bulls and youths performing together, which fascinated me. How I wish I could have observed those strange ancient rites, the grace and agility of the dancers set off by the strength and ferocity of their partners. Surely these were all children of the Minotaur, before he fell to Theseus.

How much kinder those rites seem, if pictured truly, than the blood sacrifice required by the rites of Mithras.

On another expedition we traveled to North Africa, where Hadrian reviewed the troops, drilled along with them in the merciless heat, and gave them a rousing speech before departing to embark on a lion hunt. On that occasion, Hadrian declared me too inexperienced to participate, which I found humiliating, because I knew he was right. I kept to myself in the encampment as much as possible, hating the inescapable dust and dry heat and listening to the rustle of strange animals which gathered by the water hole's edge at night, looming out of the darkness beyond our camp like ghosts. I would have liked to observe them, but the danger of encountering a lion prevented that opportunity.

BACK IN ITALY once again, we camped out during a boar hunt in the Tuscan countryside, where our local guide unearthed strange edible fungi resembling shriveled black hearts that tasted of the Great Mother's breath, exhaled. (I saved a couple of these to take with me with the intention of giving one to my grandparents' old cook, still living at home in Bithynia, whenever we next traveled there.)

A mosquito managed to slip through the netting of the tent where we slept one night, and hovered, emitting its ominous buzz. The imp landed on my arm, where I could see it by candlelight. I smacked, and a droplet of blood burst across my bare skin.

"Got me, too," Hadrian said, rubbing at a welt that already had begun to swell and redden on his left shoulder.

I inspected the squashed and bloody remnant and held out my forearm to my lover.

"Well, then," I said, "I fear I've just swatted our only son and heir."

He laughed, regarding that tiny smear on my flesh where our blood for a moment commingled.

EVERYWHERE WE VENTURED throughout the Empire, I saw immediately how the soldiers and veterans, of the Dacian wars especially, revered Hadrian, who had served with various legions during his youthful military career. They consider him one of their own, for whenever he led troops into battle, he stayed in the field with his men and fought alongside them, asking nothing of them which he did not first ask of himself. Any leader worth his salt must do so, according to Hadrian. Through their loyalty and admiration, I learned to better comprehend Hadrian's own love of discipline, valor, and bravery—strengths that contrast his quick blood.

To his credit, he has worked at constraining his natural tendency to anger. But at times, circumstance and the pressures inherent to his position undermine his self-control.

Once, after a morning in Rome spent meeting with a quarrelsome delegation of spice merchants, we were at lunch, just a small gathering of his most intimate friends and attendants.

One of the servants, a crone no bigger than a sparrow, knocked over Hadrian's wine glass while reaching to set a platter of grapes and figs on the table before him. Most of the wine spilled into his plate. Some dribbled down the tablecloth into his lap. He turned and slapped at her. It was a casual blow, but one that dropped her to the floor. She swayed there for a moment, and then stood up again.

He did not notice, having turned to push his plate further away from the table's edge and call for a fresh one, but I saw how tears of mortification sprang into her eyes while she backed away and bowed, apologizing.

I was furious that he could be so callous with someone old and fragile, over what was so clearly an accident, and furious at myself as well, for my inability to speak up. I wasn't brave enough to chastise the emperor for fear of what he might do to me in turn.

Later that same afternoon, I went along with him to inspect a new shipment of wild animals arriving in port from Africa to be transported to the amphitheatre. In one large cage, stinking of carrion, a lion and a lioness lay enclosed with two cubs that rolled and tumbled and cuffed each other, refereed by the female while the male ignored them. I chose that moment to make up for my earlier failure of conscience.

"Don't you find it interesting," I said, "how the lion feels no need to demonstrate his strength to those cubs, even when they try to annoy him. He knows he could kill them with one swipe of his paw, and that's enough. He holds his strength and ferocity in reserve, and sheathes his claws before the little ones, who hold no threat for him."

Standing before that crate of bronze captives, I stared at Hadrian's face in profile until he turned and looked back at me.

I held his gaze for some time. I believe he caught my meaning, because he never again struck another servant in my presence. He did strike me once, but that involved another matter. I know he will regret it for the rest of his life.

DURING ANOTHER OF our winters spent in Athens, where I turned seventeen while workers finished rebuilding the temple of Zeus there under Hadrian's orders, the majority of our time became given over to philosophical discussion and the making of music, a preoccupation Hadrian enjoyed but seldom allowed himself when in Rome, where it seemed suspect, too frivolous—too Greek. By this time, due to all the traveling, my formal education at the school had ceased, although he gave me permission to avail myself of any of the philosophers at court for tutoring.

THAT WINTER, HADRIAN introduced me to another old friend of his, Flavius Arrianus, a fellow Bithynian with whom I had the distinct pleasure of conversing in our original tongue. The fetters eased from my thoughts as my speech fell into its old familiar flow. As excellent as Hadrian's Greek is, his tongue is no match for a native's.

Arrian treated me with kindness and a certain delicacy, arising from both our shared geographic origins and my relationship with Hadrian. (I suspect Arrian also may have served as a catamite in times past.) No doubt others at court had made fun of his rustic roots as well, at least until he took up his stylus and silenced his critics. Talent, like love and bird shit, strikes where it pleases. Arrian often spoke to me of his favorite hound, gentle and quick and blessed with grey eyes, so I suggested he write about her, that others also might have the pleasure of hearing about her.

When we met, Arrian had just spent two years collecting the sayings of Epictetus before the aged Stoic philosopher died. Hadrian expressed an interest in this project, for as a young man, long before becoming emperor, he had met Epictetus during his own first visit to Athens, and engaged in a dialogue with the philosopher.

Hadrian related to us from memory, no doubt word for word or nearly so, some of their discourse, which had consisted of Hadrian asking questions, Epictetus answering. Arrian copied their conversation while the emperor repeated it for us. I, too, wrote down a few of their exchanges, ones that most intrigued me:

"What is a man?"

"Similar to a bath: the first room is the tepidarium, the warm bath, in which infants are born thoroughly anointed; the second room, the sudatorium, the sweat-room, is boyhood; the third room is the assa, the dry-room, the preference of youth; the fourth room, the frigi-darium, the cold bath, is appropriate to old age, in which sense comes to all."

"What are stars?"

"The destiny of humans."

"What is the sea?"

"The way of doubt."

"What is a boat?"

"A wondering house."

"What is sleep?"

"An image of death."

"What is love?"

"The annoyance of heart's leisure, shamefulness in boys, reddening in virgins, fury in women, ardor in youth, laughter in age, it is worthlessness in the mocking of fault."

"What is a sacrifice?"

"A lessening."

"What is without fellowship?"

"Kingship."

"What is a king?"

"A piece of the gods."

"What is Rome?"

"The fount of authority of the sphere of the earth, mother of nations, possessor of things, the common-dwelling of the Romans, consecration of eternal peace."

"What is the best life?"

"The shortest one."

"What thing is most certain?"

"Death."

"What is death?"

"Perpetual security."

"What is death?"

"The fearing of many, if the wise man lives, inimical to life, the spirit of the living, the dread of parents, the spoils of freedom, the cause of testaments, the conversation after destruction, the end of woefulness, the forgetfulness after memory, the leading torch, the load of burial, the inscription of a monument; death is the end of all evil."

During that winter in Athens Hadrian and Arrian also discussed Alexander, for Hadrian intended to visit the great man's tomb upon traveling to Alexandria, a trip he felt he needed to make soon. I renewed my acquaintance with other writers and philosophers at the court, and heard about the suicide of Euphrates, a Stoic philosopher, as well. This event troubled me, and stayed on my mind for some time.

Euphrates, frail and elderly and suffering from a liver ailment, had come to the decision that he wanted to kill himself in the traditional manner, by drinking hemlock. He also decided that, as a matter of ethical behavior and simple courtesy, he must first ask permission of Hadrian—since the act would, perforce, oblige an end of his services to the emperor's court.

He sent word to Hadrian of his intention, with a request that he be allowed to carry it out. I believe he knew permission would be granted, but formally submitted this final request so he could proceed with a clear conscience, and without inconveniencing the emperor by an unexpected death.

After receiving this permission, the philosopher attended dinner as usual and behaved in his normal manner, even making small jokes and laughing at others. I did not see how a man could behave in so natural a fashion when he meant to take his own life soon. I believed he would have to seem withdrawn, or sad, or full of emotion.

One of the Stoics explained to me that his suicide was a rational act, and thus Euphrates behaved in a rational manner during his final hours. It was not an act of emotional turmoil, despite its origin in physical pain. A Stoic might endure all things—yet also might choose not to, after consideration.

Hadrian seemed somber when he discussed this event with me, but he believed Euphrates had exercised his right as a citizen. He didn't realize what an impact the Stoic's choice made on me. Euphrates' ending of his life by his own hand, the making of such a decision and the act of will behind it, preoccupied my mind for some time, even after we packed up again to travel to Sicily, and then on to Phrygia.

During a visit to the tomb of Alcibiades, Hadrian ordered a new marble statue to honor the beloved hero and his fallen companion, and we stayed on to participate in the local feasting, horse racing, and dancing that accompanied the announcement of the memorial's refurbishment. Late in the night, while the fire waned, all the company sang and played instruments. I ventured to offer up a song of my own. The look of pleased surprise on Hadrian's face touched me, and made me realize just how far down in my own thoughts I had been wandering, alone, like Persephone maundering through Hades. I vowed to quit dwelling in contemplation of death, and to attack my personal studies with renewed vigor whenever we arrived again in Rome.

As it happened, we returned in time for Plotina's funeral.

Though he did not mention it, I suspect Hadrian may have felt some guilt for not having been at her side during her final illness. Despite the Senate patricians' disdain for the staid old custom, Hadrian wore a black toga for the full nine days of mourning in tribute to his adoptive mother and mentor. He scrupled over Plotina's apotheosis and burial ceremonies and insisted on every formality in his bestowal of posthumous honors upon her. He commissioned a temple in her memory in Nemausus in Gaul, just as he had commissioned a temple for the Deified Trajan, the only one of his public works Hadrian ever chose to have his name carved upon—proof of his rightful succession set in stone.

Plotina's ashes were interred with her husband's beneath his column at the foot of Quirinal Hill. Grief etched new lines in Hadrian's face.

Next, he focused on completion of the new temple of Venus and Rome, and consulted with Apollodorus, the prominent architect, about his plans for a great temple he intended to consecrate to Pan and all other gods, known and unknown, as well.

Hadrian decided to revise the plans for the Pantheon himself, so that the building assumed a spherical shape, with a dome open at its center to provide light to the interior. He commissioned a variety of marble and granite from quarries all over Italy, Greece, Egypt and Africa to grace the new home of the gods. The effect was beautiful.

I loved to stand in the center of its polished expanse of floor and look up at that oculus which let in the sky like the eye of heaven, a porthole for Zeus. The white marble exterior and bronze dome dazzled viewers' eyes in the sunshine. At night, beneath the moonlight, the marble seemed to glow. When it stormed, showers of droplets patterned the marble floor below the open space and the sweet smell of rain rose like incense beneath the heavens rumbling with thunder.

Even Hadrian's wife Sabina, newly appointed with the title of empress relinquished by Plotina in death, attended the ceremonies for the opening of the temples.

Though he dislikes her, Hadrian would never consider embarrassing Sabina publicly by divorcing her. He once even banished a writer and historian, Seutonius, from court because of the man's inexcusable rudeness to her, out of respect for her position. But he always preferred the company of Plotina, and even that of his mother-in-law, Matidia, to that of his wife. I suspect the feeling was mutual.

To me, Sabina seems almost put away in lavender now, surrounded by her attendants and chosen companions. For several years she has sequestered herself at her own villa, making only those official appearances required by protocol. She strikes me as a lonely woman, though perhaps she likes the perquisites of her role well enough. She has always remained civil, even gracious, to me. Perhaps she doesn't understand the nature of my relationship with her husband. Or, perhaps, doesn't care. I sometimes wondered whether she wanted children, or regrets not having them. What else is there for a woman, even if she is a queen?

Hadrian himself seems unconcerned that he has no natural-born heirs. After all, he was adopted by his imperial predecessor, just as Trajan was adopted by Nerva before him. When the time comes, he intends to follow suit.

AFTER PLOTINA'S DEATH, mindful of his own mortality, Hadrian decided to begin work on his own tomb, on the far bank of the Tiber. He and Apollodorus have often sparred over that particular architectural project. Apollodorus feels invalidated by the amateur, and Hadrian feels envious of the professional. Apollodorus might do well to recall that, while he is the professional, Hadrian is the emperor. At the least, he might refrain from comparing Hadrian's drawings of dome elevations to pumpkins.

Perhaps to spite the architect, Hadrian ordered that Trajan's bridge over the river Ister, designed by Apollodorus, be dismantled during a period of border realignment and fortification.

Hadrian also criticized Trajan's victory column as unseemly, whereas I found its original friezes possess, despite clumsy execution, a certain energy or vitality not always found in Roman copies of Greek style—although I did not, of course, venture to offer this dissent aloud.

Thinking to improve my understanding of engineering and architecture, I asked Hadrian's permission to study higher mathematics while we were back in residency in the court at Rome. I found I could follow the threads of the mathematician's logic for a while, and began to see a pattern emerging from its weaving. There are patterns within patterns, patterns to be discerned everywhere if one but looks for them, and the thought of all these smaller patterns incorporated into one enormous pattern occurred to me—but then the thread snarled, the numbers blurred, and that final design I could not bring myself to grasp fell away into tangles. A little frightened by the experience, I gave up, and thanked the tutor for his graciousness in trying to teach me.

Meanwhile, Hadrian, having been taunted as a young man for his own provincial Latin accent, worried that I didn't apply myself hard enough to learning more about Latin, didn't exert myself to unlock all of its intricacies, grammatical and otherwise, and perfect my pronunciation.

But why should I? I have Greek. Latin: language of government, formality, classification, officialdom. Greek: language of the mind, the soul, poetry, philosophy, medicine—in short, the language of life. Any Roman writer worthy of that appellation has looked to the Greeks before him, dipped in and borrowed well, whether Virgil

looking back to Homer's poems for his *Aeneid*, or Julius
Caesar emulating Xenophon in the history of his cam-
paigns. That foundation is the one on which I stand.

DURING MY SPAN of time as the emperor's favorite, I
found myself exposed to many an intrigue, vendetta, and
scandal at the imperial court. Yet my own betrayal came,
oddly enough, from within the nest of my family back
home in Claudiopolis.

When word arrived of my grandfather's death,
Hadrian gave me the news. Upon his inquiries into my
family's situation, he gleaned additional bad news: it
seemed my inheritance had evaporated.

"Your Uncle Thersites," Hadrian said, "has managed
the family investments and properties in such a way that
there will be nothing remaining of the estate to be passed
along to you."

"Not even the house?"

"Not even the house. It will be sold when your grandmother dies."

At least my grandmother might continue to live
there, facing down her own death. Hadrian fumed on
my behalf, which I found both dismaying and gratify-
ing. Now, of course, I realize his anger arose from his
superior understanding of the situation—that when
we parted, upon my coming of age, I could no longer
count on any resources of my own to fall back upon.

When we traveled to Bithynia, my name now linked
with Hadrian's on every man's lips all over Claudiopolis,
I witnessed my uncle's extreme discomfort upon his introduction to Hadrian. When the two men clasped hands,
Hadrian sized him up with a hard gaze and a soft "Ah,

yes," and then dismissed him, right there in his own house.

I derived a certain pleasure, I confess, from seeing my uncle's face cloud and fall when the understanding settled upon him that the emperor knew of the estate situation. Any aspirations he harbored toward a higher post in the government were hopeless.

Nonetheless, I felt ashamed that my family had thus been tarnished in Hadrian's eyes, and even felt a little sorry for my uncle, a likeable fellow who could not have foreseen how his own plans and ambitions might someday be thwarted due to the chance meeting of his nephew and the emperor of Rome. I could never bring myself to believe he had siphoned away all those funds and assets on purpose, despite Hadrian's own thoughts on the matter.

With my grandmother, Hadrian waxed gracious. Sitting there in the atrium of my old home, he asked her about my childhood, encouraged her to hold forth on local myths and superstitions, and even told stories of his own about the tribulations of being emperor, while I kept silent, savoring her pleasure.

"Once I found myself petitioned for a second time by the same man," he said, "only the fellow had dyed his hair black since our first exchange. When his turn in line came, I told him I could see a strong family resemblance, for I felt sure I already spoke to his grandfather."

My grandmother laughed, covering her mouth with her palm. A remnant of girlish beauty radiated from her face in that moment, the sun peering from behind a cloud and then retreating once more.

"Another time," Hadrian said, "I visited the public bath of a city while on a tour. There I found a man scratching his back against the lintel post outside the entrance, too poor even to go in for a bath. Feeling sympathy for his plight, I decided to give him a slave to scratch his back, and money enough to feed and bathe the both of them."

My grandmother nodded, waiting for him to continue.

"The next day, when once again I went to the baths, wouldn't you know—a whole flock of old men were waiting around the entrance, rubbing against the posts for all they were worth. They looked astonished, not to mention disappointed, when I merely suggested they might have a try at scratching one another."

She and Hadrian both laughed.

During that trip home, I also gave the old cook her first taste of a truffle, that culinary oddity from beneath the Tuscan woods I had saved for her. When I stepped into her kitchen, she exclaimed over me, how tall, how handsome. When I held out my hand, she took the spongy black lump without hesitation.

"What's this now?" She turned it around between her thumb and forefinger.

I held out a knife and said, "Taste it."

She pared off a sliver, sniffed it, closed her eyes and popped the bit into her mouth. When she opened her eyes again, they looked liquid. She closed her fist around the rest of it, as if she were burying treasure.

"Ah, Antinous," she said. "Thank you."

UPON OUR RETURN to Rome, I learned that Korias, no longer ensconced in the court, had converted to Christianity and left his government post in order to follow his new faith off into the wild, perhaps somewhere in Africa. Although we settled on friendship in school, I still sometimes wished I had slept with him just once, all night, my hand on his cock, my head on his heart.

Of course I heard the rumors, everyone has, of the atrocities committed by that cult, how they drown children in baptismal rites, drink blood and eat human flesh in order to make themselves immortal, and hold frenzied orgies in secret chambers underground. Having known Korias, however, I never believed them. The followers of Jesus of Nazareth claim their own leader offered himself as a sacrifice for anyone, not just those of Jewish origin, who wishes for his intercession with Yahweh, who is, they claim, also his father. One day he will open up the underworld, they say, so that all the dead may fly out. I sometimes wonder whether Korias himself did not have rather a taste for self-sacrifice. It seems so, now, to me.

AMYRRA HAD NOTICED a couple of dark hairs that now shadowed my upper lip upon our return to Rome. She made a gift to me in secret: a pair of tweezers.

"Just—like that," she said, and demonstrated by tugging a stray hair from her own brow. "Pluck, pluck for luck, Antinous. Remember, you are suffering for beauty."

She handed the implement over to me and held up a mirror so I could look into it. I caught up a filament of hair in the tweezers' tapered jaws and pulled. That first sting surprised me, but I began to tweeze above my lip and along my chin almost daily to preserve the nudity of youth—a vain attempt to forestall the inevitable.

To immortalize my youthful beauty, Hadrian had engaged a couple of artists and sculptors to capture my likeness for a few works of art he planned to install at his Tibur villa. I soon grew accustomed to their constant scrutiny. Even when I wasn't sitting for a portrait, as often as not some man sat off to one side of me during a banquet or some other gathering, sketching my features, his own brow beetled with concentration.

For as long as I had known Hadrian he had been designing and overseeing the restoration and expansion of his country villa at Tibur, east of the great city, situated so that the sun always appeared to set on Rome. The original house, acquired as part of his wife's inheritance, dated back to the Republic. That venerable structure was first refurbished, and then encompassed in its entirety within the newer, grander main structure. He also built a villa in miniature upon an island within the grounds, for use as his private retreat.

I always enjoyed walking the grounds there, trying to envision the planned Academy in its completion, wreathed with art, or the dome of the tower intended to house an observatory for his perusal of the stars. Plotina always had enjoyed strolling there, as had Matidia, Hadrian's mother-in-law. Sabina herself seldom visited.

Once I suggested to him that he might commemorate his travels by construction of temples or other monuments evocative of the great cities under his command.

"You might place a miniature Parthenon on that hill," I said, nodding toward the swell of ground that rose beneath a grove of oaks, "to recall the Acropolis. And perhaps a long reflecting pool near the spring to represent the Nile." I knew how he looked forward to traveling in Egypt, and in particular to a visit to Alexandria.

"A child's notion," he said, but smiled. "Some statuary might be appropriate, at that—cats, crocodiles, the eye of Horus."

When next he met with the architects, builders and stonemasons, I noticed he had followed some of my suggestions, but I said nothing. I understood him better by then, and I needed no recognition from them.

The last time we visited the villa, I discovered a favorite mosaic among all the new works, a Centaur hurling a stone at a striped, snarling tiger.

Upon its completion, Hadrian's villa compound will rival any imperial palace for splendor, for it will boast almost a thousand rooms, and even an underground passageway for servants and service wagons. There the emperor and company might enjoy the countryside undisturbed, far from the demands of Rome and the baleful eyes of the Senate. The senators' refusal to acknowledge Hadrian's superiority as ruler galls him, although he never has spoken of it to me. The villa will provide a respite from his lack of popularity with certain patricians in the city and at court.

THOSE AT COURT who gave me credit for good behavior in those days did not perceive a shameful truth I understood about myself. My apparent detachment masked a fierce attachment to my own concerns (which included anything that might concern my emperor and lover). It also masqueraded adequately enough as compassion and affection, and made it easier to avoid those power games which preoccupy so many minds at court, causing it at times to resemble a nest of adders.

I felt no curiosity or interest in gossip about events which seemed to intrigue others. I simply could not care less who slept with whom, or who despised this or that one. What I did find fascinating: the intrigue process itself.

Once an accusation got into the air, say, that a certain man neglected his aged parents, or slept with another's wife, the accused was judged in the court of gossip and hearsay, and most often found guilty, convicted by everyone around him without a shred of empirical proof having been offered. Watching this process unfold over and over again throughout various scandals at court made me realize why our laws have come about—not only to prosecute the guilty, once they are determined based on factual evidence, but also, to protect the innocent from foes and false friends happy to seize any excuse to bring about their ruin.

I found it fascinating as well to see how those who think of themselves as good citizens, having decided that another has transgressed and violated some social boundary, feel free therefore to transgress against him, to violate with impunity that individual's own boundaries in ways heretofore undreamed of—making nasty comments, observations, and jokes at his expense, and often in a manner calculated to further insult him by intimating he can't possibly understand he is the butt of their humor. His right to privacy and decency are somehow revoked, though no evidence to prove his guilt has been found, and very well never may be. Yet he shall remain guilty in public memory.

At such times, I kept apart from the crowd as much as possible; held my tongue; remained polite especially toward those who scorned and stung me, and willingly played the fool to please any who wished to outsmart me. No man is offended by the impression that you think him the wiser of the two of you, since, in secret, he inevitably believes this to be true.

Many assumed that because I was young and naïve, I must be so to the point of stupidity. I never exerted myself to correct this false impression, for seldom is one hurt more by such underestimation than by an accurate or exaggerated assessment—as long as one is careful not to return this favor to one's detractors.

And I never lied. But truth, from different angles, may vary.

Some at court sought to undermine me, mistaken in their idea that I possessed any real power by association with Hadrian, while others sought to use me to draw closer to him. Both sorts thought to use me to relay their messages.

"Please tell Hadrian this" or "Hadrian might be interested to know that" flew in one of my ears and out the other. I said nothing, hostile or otherwise, to those who would make me their errand-boy, but simply declined to relay such messages unless I perceived any information therein which might be of use to him.

Others sought to get me drunk, hoping I might reveal Hadrian's secrets to them. In vino veritas, per Pliny. The truth is, I can hold my wine, and take care to water it well besides, so that particular strategy, found to be ineffectual, soon fell into disuse.

For the most part, I found it prudent to keep exchanges pared to the lightest oiling of pleasantries required to skim the surface of court relations. I became

adept at mouthing platitudes in lieu of providing information, rather like an oracle: What benefits one province
benefits all. A stout wind fills all sails, and the rising tide
bears all boats upon its shoulder.

As a rule, when entering the palace and other imperial or public buildings, I stayed well away from balco-
nies, ledges, and steep stairwells, in order to prevent any
danger to Hadrian, or myself, of falling or being shoved
down, as well as to avoid confronting that part of myself
which always felt tempted to jump, or push.

THERE AT COURT in Rome again I found my old nemesis,
Marcus. I believed he still hated me for knowing what
he had been, a bully who elbowed his way through the
schoolyard. A cruel boy, and greedy, the sort who steals
the coins from the tongues of dead men. I thought I must
stay on guard, never find myself alone with him. I did not
know, indeed none of the court yet realized, how ill he
was already, beset by a wasting disease, which in time left
him coughing up blood, staining with deeper crimson the
scarlet of his hand cloths.

Wandering about the city one afternoon in late
spring, heading in the direction of the Forum, I came
upon Marcus while he, too, strolled about at leisure. His
face was covered by a sun mask, a mixture of flour, egg
white, and olive oil. One of his attendants shaded him
with a fringe-trimmed parasol.

Catching sight of me, he put up a hand and stopped
his own procession.

"Antinous, what are you thinking. You must protect your skin when you go out. Where's your mask?
You should at least be wearing a hat," he said, chiding

my carelessness. I resented such invasive concern for my complexion as much as I resented his usual tone of superiority.

"Thank you, Marcus," I said, "but I have never minded a little sun."

He squinted at me, shading his eyes with one palm, and sighed for effect.

"Fine. Please yourself then, country mouse, but don't say I didn't warn you. Some day you may regret soaking up all that sunshine."

He nodded to his attendant, and they proceeded in the other direction.

LUCIUS COMMODUS STILL remained among my enemies at court. He preferred to attack one in public, in front of a crowd, hoping to get others to join him and gang up on the intended victim.

Once, after a banquet, when the wine-stoked discussion turned to the frequent topic of the ideal relationship and whether or not it must include spiritual love, respect, and physical love, Commodus, seeing an opportunity to remind me and everyone else of my inferior status, hastened to stick his barb in while feigning a post-dinner languidness, lolling about on his couch.

"Relationships between members of different classes can never include real love. Wouldn't you all agree?" He waved away a platter of fruit proffered by a servant girl as if swatting at a fly.

"How can there be true respect between men who cannot fully grasp each other's milieu? Love without respect is a lame horse, and of course, one mustn't ride it.

111

Wouldn't you agree, Antinous?"

"What you say is true, Commodus," I said. I lifted the apple I had taken from the platter, inspected it, feigning carelessness of my own. "Yet respect without love may well be a dead horse, and one cannot ride it, either. Love and respect belong in tandem, alive and well and pulling in harness together, don't you agree?"

I held the apple up to my mouth and crunched it between my teeth.

Hadrian laughed at this response and slapped me on the shoulder. Then he turned to Commodus and slapped him on his.

"Commodus, old friend," he said, "One must always take care not to place bets on the wrong horse."

Commodus gave a weak laugh and glared at me before turning away to seek fresh conversation elsewhere.

Hadrian, of course, felt gratified by our squabbling, pleased as any harlot who pits her would-be lovers against one another for a show to amuse herself and her friends before deigning at last to give one the nod. Later that night, as if to rub salt into the stripes where Commodus had lacerated my pride, Hadrian told me he planned to invite him on the trip to Alexandria.

"He most likely will become my heir," he said. "Plotina and I discussed it more than once, and I believe she would agree with my decision."

"I'm sure she would," I said, and then pulled the blanket over my head, not wishing to discuss Commodus any longer, and burrowed deeper into the bedclothes.

I MISS SEVERAL of my friends from the court of Rome, including a court physician, Marcellus Sidetes, of whom

I've grown quite fond, now that I understand his character. Although brilliant, he mistakes the exercising of a needle-sharp tongue for wit, and then seems puzzled when those punctured by his jabs dislike and avoid his company. And such jabs are the worse for being astute and true—no man enjoys having his faults, character flaws, and shortcomings pointed out, most often having become all too aware of them already via self-examination.

My grandmother, when I was small, used to say, "You catch more flies with a drop of honey than with a jar of vinegar." I always thought that truth self-evident, but have come to realize that for some, like Marcellus, it is not clear at all.

Once I realized no malice lay behind Marcellus' remarks, I vowed to get past that sharpness, befriend and learn from him. When he found my interest in his field to be sincere, Marcellus talked with me at length of modern medical practice, and lamented the burning of the library in Alexandria, which had destroyed, among countless other precious documents, many important medical treatises.

I learned that he, too, is a writer. He is working on a poem of some length on medical remedies, *Chironides*, which he hopes may find a place in Hadrian's library someday. He also is writing a treatise regarding werewolves, their diagnosis and treatment. I persuaded him to allow me to read a little of his work about this malady, which I found fascinating. The affliction known as lycanthropy, or cynanthropy, causes its victims to go out by night during the month of February, hanging about tombs and behaving like dogs or wolves until morning returns, leaving them hollow-eyed, dry-tongued, listless, and thirsty.

"One must recognize that lycanthropy is a form of melancholia," Marcellus wrote, and he outlined a particular regimen of treatment he believed might prove successful, including the use of opium to help the afflicted ones sleep.

Marcellus also discussed with me the success rates for various experimental procedures being tried on injured gladiators, and confessed that he wonders whether dissection ought to be allowed on the human body (only after the owner is deceased, he emphasized—unlike Herophilus and Erasistratus, doctors of old who once practiced their anatomical experiments on criminals, still alive, in Alexandria).

"Animal anatomy is similar to ours, yet there are still differences which may lead physicians to draw false conclusions about men after studying animals," he said to me once. "We are just another species of animal, after all—when you cut a man open, he stinks."

ALL IN ALL, this life in the imperial court has been quite an education—more than I ever expected in many ways, but also, in certain ways, less. For how dismaying it is to find oneself buffeted at all times by others' never-ending quests for power, to be forced to witness man's cruelty to man, even prevailed upon to participate in it—when, after all, one wanted only to seek out love, truth, beauty, the hidden perfection of Forms.

FIRE

III. Fire

THE OBJECT OF his affection. His beloved. Does anyone question whether the beloved loves in return? Does the beloved have any choice?

Socrates, it is said, once claimed as his gift the ability to pick out at once the lover and the beloved. When Hadrian looks upon me now, he fancies he sees the face of his beloved. He does not. Like Narcissus gazing into the pool, he sees his own youth, Publius Aelius Hadrianus, reflected. That is what he loves.

That is what he looks for now when he orders my image recreated over and over in paintings and sculpture, disguised now as Dionysos, now as Ganymede, Hermes, Pan, Adonis, paying homage to his ideal of beauty—if he were honest, he would have me made in his own image, draped in his own purple toga.

He has defined me to suit himself within the dyad of our relationship; by ascribing to me certain characteristics and virtues, he also has denied me myriad others. Just as he measures all creatures against an ideal Form, Hadrian has held me up to his ideal Form—as he no doubt also assessed Commodus and various others before me—and found a lack of perfection.

And what will become of the one who, once the first bloom is past, no longer reflects his glory? Already, the curls of boyhood are gone, my shorn hair grown back thicker and coarser, cheek and jowl pebbled with the shadow of a beard coming on. When I become a man, this face will become the tomb of youth and beauty.

Men always believe their own love to be eternal, unchanging, unending, and so men are fools. I am not fooled, but then I am not yet a man in love.

LAST YEAR FOR my eighteenth birthday, I was given a new servant, the Caledonian slave girl Calliria, to assist me as I saw fit. I also received many new garments, a white toga such as men put on, and tunics and robes in cotton, linen, and wool, some with intricate designs embroidered on their sleeves and hems, gifts from Hadrian and others at court.

Favorinus, ever the agitator, delighted in the opportunity provided by my birthday feast to pay a visit to the court in Rome. He brought me a new pair of sandals, crafted to be both elegant and sturdy. When we had a moment to talk together during the banquet, he said, "And what are your plans now?" He cocked an eyebrow at me, and popped a grape into his mouth.

"What do you mean?"

I reached over and pulled a grape from the cluster he held.

"I mean, what do you plan to do, Antinous, when the sun hides behind the clouds, when you no longer reign as favorite? I hear your inheritance vanished with the wind.

Every courtesan needs a contingency plan, against the inevitable day."

"I'm no courtesan," I said, and knew blood flared in my cheeks already.

Favorinus patted my arm. "I don't mean to upset you, my friend. But we are, all of us, courtesans here—though only Amyrra admits it, since her gender makes it obvious."

I changed the subject.

"I never thanked you, Favorinus. For that ointment you once suggested. It did indeed work well."

"Dear boy, think nothing of it. Glad to be of help. Just remember to pass the recipe on to the next favorite."

He gave me a knowing look, then turned away to greet someone.

Favorinus regaled Hadrian and the rest of the company that evening with a reading from his rival Polemo's treatise on physiognomy, the science of deducing a man's character from the study of his physical traits and attributes, and he gave quite a performance, mincing and simpering and exaggerating his facial expressions throughout to enhance our enjoyment. I felt glad Polemo, away visiting his hometown of Smyrna, wasn't there to witness it, for no doubt an argument would have ensued.

"Oh, listen," Favorinus said, "and see if you can guess who is being described thus.

"'He was libidinous and dissolute beyond all bounds. A bulbous brow, flabby cheeks, wide mouth, a gangling scraggly neck, fat calves, and fleshy feet. His voice was like a woman's, and likewise his extremities and other bodily parts were uniformly soft; nor did he walk with an upright posture; his joints and limbs were lax. He took great care of his abundant tresses, rubbed ointments on his body, and cultivated everything that excites the desire for coitus and lust—'"

Interrupting himself, his face almost bursting with ill-concealed hilarity and annoyance, Favorinus said, "Yes, friends, indeed it is I."

Then, unscrolling the papyrus with a flourish to a section further down, he said, "And now let us hear just a brief description of the orbs of our exalted ruler.

"'Certainly the eyes of the Emperor Hadrian were of this kind: full of lovely radiance, swift, and sharp of glance. No man has ever been seen endowed with eyes more full of light.'"

To which Hadrian responded, in a dry aside that elicited laughter all around, "How nice to know one is considered well endowed."

THE NEXT MORNING, thinking she might not find it dis-agreeable on her first day in my service, I asked Calliria to take charge of my clothing. She nodded, and carried off a basketful to the cauldrons to be laundered. She was tall, with a fox-sharp face above limbs long and clean as a boy's, and moved with exceptional grace.

Late in the afternoon, when she returned with dried clothes folded into neat parcels, I asked her wash my back for me. I had sweated through my tunic, for the day was warm, and wished to change into a fresh one. The male servant who helped me bathe every morning already had gone out to take a wine-stained toga to the fuller's and run a few other errands around the city.

Calliria looked reluctant, but took the sponge and scoured it across my shoulder blades and down my spine with such vigor I felt glad she wasn't armed with a strigil. Then she turned away and set the sponge down, and started to pick up her laundry basket.

"You missed a bit below my shoulder blades on both sides," I said. "And this tunic needs to be aired out before it's worn again."

I held it out for her to tend.

She looked at the tunic, looked at me, then picked up the sponge and held it before me, not quite succeeding in concealing a look of disgust.

"Perhaps you may prefer to rewash yourself, then, sir, since your man isn't here, and I seem to have done nothing right so far in serving you."

I felt anger crawl up my neck, though begrudging admiration also stirred at her outburst; most people wouldn't dare speak in such a tone to the emperor's favorite, especially not servants. I knew I must not let such insolence go unanswered.

"How dare you talk back. Next time, I'll have you whipped."

She ducked her head, lowered her grey eyes, but not before I caught a reflection of my face in them, and an anger that mirrored my own.

Later that night, in examining my conscience I was forced to admit I felt tempted to strike, punish her, exert my power (which was only a reflection of the emperor's, of course) just because I might. So it seemed I, too, had been seduced by power, that tyrant which, in its insidious way, drains integrity from a man like an egg sucked away through a pin hole in the shell. Disgusted by my own thoughts of petty vengeance, I reminded myself of all the horrors inflicted by corrupt rulers and high-ranking officials upon those who displeased them: Christians lit up like candles, slaves torn to pieces and fed to dogs and eels, or that Asian widow I once heard about, punished for refusing to give herself in marriage to a general who wanted her.

The general, like many men, could not stand for anything to be at once beautiful and beyond reach; if necessary, the beautiful thing must be maimed or killed to maintain an illusion of control. So to teach her that beauty was only skin-deep, the general decided to have her flayed like Marsyas. Then he went the gods one better. She would skin herself. On his order, a soldier made incisions at her clavicles, told her to peel. A proud woman, she refused to scream. She got to one breast before she died.

THE NEXT AFTERNOON, watching my grey-eyed slave whose hair shrieked of battle-axe and flame as she ranged about my quarters stowing away clean clothing and gathering what was soiled, a frenzy of lust overcame me, Dionysos overpowering my senses.

Grace, nerve, pride: If she were a citizen, I might have loved her. But no female is capable of inspiring the highest form of love. The senses may fool one at times, however, into mistaking base lust for that purer emotion. One must guard against such corruption at all costs. Yet somehow, that day, my defenses failed us both.

I pulled her to me, embraced her, bent her over the low table, shoving books and papers aside to make space, hitching up the skirts of her robe and tunic to free her fine hips and buttocks. She tolerated my urgency, but did not respond.

Afterward, I expected her to avert her face and slink from my presence as any Greek or Roman servant girl might have done. Instead, she turned to me, our eyes almost level, and when her gaze met mine, a strange thing happened: It was I who broke first, looked away, then down, then back into her face, while a new feeling churned through my gut. It was, I realized, shame.

With a noticeable effort to keep her voice as level as her gaze, she said to me, "Where I live, men ask."

She spoke again, her gutter Latin grating my ears, her chin in the air, defiant.

"In my country, women are not possessions. They choose."

Her voice evoked an image that disturbed me— long, naked limbs entwined with some blue-tattooed barbarian's.

"I apologize," I heard myself say. "It will not happen again."

Later, I found myself growing furious again. Imagine a barbarian, a slave girl, demanding respect. Thinking that she matters. A coarser man would have slit her throat as soon as fucked her and rolled her into the Tiber. No doubt, she wished to slit mine.

How dare any woman, slave or otherwise, I thought, presume to chastise a Roman citizen. No crime was committed. The only punishable offense regarding a woman is to sleep with another man's wife. And I never used force, violence. Nor was she virgin. There was no blood.

And yet, she was right to feel anger. She had no choice. I see that now. Just as I now see that I never considered the act I committed with any regard to my relationship with Hadrian. At the time, those two had no connection at all in my mind, even though she was a gift from the court—and so, from him.

A FEW MONTHS ago, I spoke to her about this latest journey, to give her time to prepare my clothes for the long foray with Hadrian into Athens, Egypt and Africa. Her words to me that evening shattered something inside me, like a glass cup dropped upon tiles.

"Perhaps," she said, folding a tunic while she stared at me with those northern eyes, "I will not serve you again."

Hers are a people who believe in prophecy, and indeed some claim to see the future before it happens. Those words expressed no regret; rather a wish, or premonition.

I had intended, before departing, to present her with a sketch I created of her, with wings like those of a butterfly emerging from her shoulder blades, a rather good likeness. Instead, I tore this handiwork to shreds and burned it that very night. Bits of papyrus reddened and fluttered, then crumpled and shrank into ash.

I FOUND NO opportunity to speak to my old friend Amyrra at the farewell banquet heralding this trip, for she chose to retire to her villa in Tuscany last year, when the first signs of wavering attention at court signaled that her charms might be fading through familiarity. Her decision to remove herself before she might be dismissed seems a wise one, an example to heed. I feel no worries for her welfare. Rumor already has a new beau in the form of a retired senator stepping up to show her about the province.

At the banquet, Marcus took the opportunity to stun me, delivering the news of his illness from the couch next to mine while the rest of the guests watched a gang of tumblers perform. Leaning close to my ear to ensure that Hadrian, reclining next to me, didn't hear, he said, "You know, Antinous, I am dying."

Turning my head to look at him, I said, "Surely not."

"Yes, I am," he said. "Of course, there's hope—one can always hope—that a cure may be effected. But I've coughed blood for a few months now, and that symptom, my doctor assures me, almost always means the disease is beyond treatment. He and my father are the only ones who know. And now, you."

I felt numb, and after a moment realized I must speak.

"I'm so sorry, Marcus. I assure you, I won't speak of this to anyone—unless you wish for me to do so."

I assumed that, for whatever reasons of his own, he wanted me to give this sad news to Hadrian. What he said next, I never anticipated.

"Thank you, Antinous," he said. "and I know I must tell Hadrian, but I wanted to tell you first, because you've been a friend. One of my best friends, in truth. What a way we've traveled from our school days."

Fumbling for a response, I hesitated and then said, "Thank you, Marcus. I had no idea you thought so well of me."

He coughed, covering his mouth with a dinner napkin, and I tried not to look, despite temptation to see if spatters of blood marred the golden square.

"I've always been fond of you, Antinous. Rather fond. And thought you might be fond of me as well—but it seemed impolitic to admit it," he said, "given the circumstances."

125

He gave a discreet nod toward Hadrian, whose eyes were still on the performers. "You understand."

"Of course," I said, feeling even more uncomfortable.

In truth, I'd always found Marcus about as alluring as a turnip. But I felt loathe to disabuse him of his false notions now, if such a belief comforted.

Marcus himself changed the subject.

"So perhaps you'll be allowed to go on the lion hunt this time out. Maybe he'll even let you have a spear."

This failed to rouse a response from me, recovering as I was from the twin blows of his illness and romantic revelation. Then he said, "Don't worry, lions much prefer Christians anyway, or so I'm told. Speaking of which—any news of Korias?"

This question at least I felt safe in answering. I noticed gooseflesh on my arms.

"No, nothing. And you?"

"Not a word," said Marcus, perhaps crestfallen at having failed to elicit any confessions, romantic or otherwise, from me. "Maybe the lions already got him."

A guest on the other side of his couch poked him in the shoulder, and began to repeat a joke he'd just heard. Marcus laughed as if nothing were amiss. I busied myself with the remains of the dinner growing cold on my plate, relieved that Hadrian didn't seem to suspect anything wrong.

Strange to say, but I have begun to see how Marcus as a boy just might have resembled a young Hadrian; how, despite all of his gifts and his status, insecurity might undermine him, reduce him to the rank of bully, and degrade him as well as his victims.

I wonder whether the gravity of his situation had caused Marcus to engage in self-examination, and allowed his better nature to unfurl, even as his days began to wind down. And I am sorry not be there, at the last, if I might have been any help to him.

MOMIUS, MY OLD stable master, seemed reluctant to let me take my leave when I stopped by to see which horses we would ride to hunt on this last trip.

He grasped my hand in his calloused one and paused for a moment. One of the stable cats minced past, intent upon some invisible prey.

"That's a good horse there, Antinous," he said of the one he'd chosen for me, pulling his hand free to wave it in the direction of Balius' stall. The horse's alert brown eyes watched us over the top of the gate, as if he intended to size me up as well. I had never ridden him before. He was the hunt master's usual mount, just as Xanthus was Hadrian's. I wondered why I was being offered the penultimate horse, and which horse the hunt master now would ride, instead.

"A good horse. So take care of him now. Don't risk him unnecessarily."

"I will, sir. I promise. I'll do my best."

"That I know, boy. That I know," he said.

Balius in his stall gave a whinny, as if he understood our conversation and approved of what he heard.

I knew this show of concern for my horse was Momius' way of expressing fondness for me. But now I also wonder whether he intended to give me warning with his oblique urgings—whether he guessed the test of courage and skill Hadrian intended for me during the upcoming hunt, and felt caught between loyalty to the emperor and concern for a former hand, toward whom he still felt a paternal affection.

When we toured in Athens again before traveling further east and south, my official designation as imperial favorite provided me with the privilege of conducting the sacrifice to the sacred Python of the oracle, to honor the emperor's genius. The wrens bred for this ceremony had been mutilated, their wings clipped to prevent flight. The drubbing of those ruined wings when I placed the creatures atop the great serpent's altar recalled to me the fluttering heart of a hare I once captured and tamed, before the hounds fell upon him and tore it out.

Once again I found myself asking why gods are so cruel as to elicit praise from fountains of gore, delight in the deaths of male and female, or find, in the shattering of skulls delicate as eggshell, a source of glee.

At the Athenian court, Arrian was persuaded to read aloud the piece I had "commissioned" regarding his favorite bitch, now expanded into an essay called "On Hunting with Hounds," which Hadrian and I both found graceful and moving. I asked for a copy of this text as a keepsake so I might re-read certain passages at my leisure, and Arrian seemed pleased to oblige, delivering the manuscript to me the next morning.

"One should sacrifice to Artemis the Huntress," he wrote, "in thanks for such a possession; and one should sacrifice also after a successful hunt, and dedicate the first-fruits of the catch to the goddess, and purify the hounds and the huntsmen, according to local tradition and custom.

"Some Celts have the custom also of making an annual sacrifice to Artemis: they display an offertory box for the goddess, and when a hare is caught they put two obols in the box, for a fox, a drachma. . .when the festival of Artemis' birth comes round, the box is opened, and from the collected sum they buy a sacrificial animal, some a sheep, some a goat, some a calf, if there is enough. After the sacrifice, and having given the first offering of the animal to the Huntress, as is the custom in various places, they and their hounds have a feast. They also put garlands on their hounds on that day, to make it clear that they are holding a festival in their honor. . ."

My favorite passage offered a description of one hunter's beloved hound:

"For I myself reared a hound with the greyest of grey eyes, and she was fast and a hard worker and spirited and agile, so that when she was young she once dealt with four hares in one day. And apart from that she is the most gentle (I still had her when I was writing this) and most fond of humans, and never previously did any other dog long to be with me and my fellow-huntsman Megillus as she does.

"If she sees one of us even after a short period of time, she jumps into the air gently, as if welcoming him, and she gives a bark with the welcome, showing her affection. When she is with one of us at dinner she touches him with her paws alternately, reminding him that she too should be given some of the food. And indeed she makes many different noises, more than any other dog that I think I have seen; and she shows audibly what she wants.

"And because when she was being trained as a puppy she was punished with a whip, if anyone to this day should mention a whip, she goes up to the one who has said it and crouches down like one beseeching, and fits her mouth to his mouth as if she is kissing, and jumps up and hangs from his neck, and does not let him go until the angry one gives up the threat. And so I think that I should not hesitate to write down the name of this dog, for it to survive her even into the future, viz. that Xenophon the Athenian had a dog called Horme, very fast and very clever and quite out of this world."

Arrian also presented me with a belated birthday gift, a silver cup commissioned from a renowned silversmith, a stunning piece of craftsmanship. The outside of the bowl had been worked in two scenes which complemented each other. One side depicted a bearded man and a youth making love with gestures at once ardent and tender, while the other showed a young man similarly engaged with a boy. I supposed the former image might have reminded Arrian of Hadrian and me, and that he assumed we might find it pleasing, but I wondered about the two figures on the other side. The boy there looked resigned, his features slack, eyes staring off into the distance.

On a jaunt into Smyrna, to address some civic concerns called to his attention by Polemo, Hadrian coerced me into spending an evening with him and a new courtesan named Hostia, one I found little better than a street prostitute. I thought her coarse in manner and appearance both, almost a different species from Amyrra, despite their common gender. Hers was a face in which all sweetness had curdled, and beneath the smoke of incense, her house smelt of rancid cheese.

Well aware of my disdain, this Hostia missed no opportunity to hiss in my ear, while pretending to whisper enticements during the wine drinking.

"You think you are superior? You are no better than I—just another plaything to be discarded once his desire is slaked. Don't put on airs with me, fancy boy."

When she led Hadrian off into her gaudy, mirror-encrusted bedroom, he turned and gestured, wanting me to follow. No doubt he intended for the three of us to engage one another, but I pretended not to understand and sank down onto a cushioned stool just inside the doorway.

I gazed around the glittering candlelit room, trying my best to ignore the two of them coupling on the low, wide bed. This proved impossible, the movement of their twining limbs drawing my gaze against my will to the naked bodies before me in reflection after reflection around the mirrored walls.

Hadrian turned her over, to take her from behind. Her breasts and pale buttocks shuddered and recoiled from the force of his thrusting, the muscles of his thighs working as he gripped her waist with one arm, bracing himself with the other.

My eyes were drawn upward to the mirror above the headboard, and there all at once I met her eyes, with their gaze of detached amusement. She had been watching me while I watched their intercourse in a state of aroused revulsion. His eyes were closed, turned inward upon himself, as always, during the act.

She flashed me a grin obscene in its complicity, insulting in its implication: "Here I am, where you usually are, and your turn is still to come."

Disgusted, I looked away. I further avenged myself by declining her after he had finished.

"Not to my taste," I said when he pressed me. Thus we disengaged Hostia and took leave of her house. Hadrian paid her a bonus as if to make up for my refusal.

His accusations later that night, whispered against my turned back, were true. I was indeed sulking. He had besmirched our sacred lust with his own base ones.

It never occurred to me that I did likewise with Calliria—perhaps even more so, for I felt some genuine emotion, angry, vengeful, regretful, toward her, rather than simple lust. My impulsive act of congress with Calliria had betrayed to me my own submerged desire for power over another, such power as Hadrian himself wields over everyone. That power becomes more of a burden and less of a privilege the longer it is possessed.

ON OUR LAST boar hunt together, during a light rain on a hillside outside Athens one afternoon, the boar I killed turned out to be the prize of the weekend. As expected, as I anticipated, my lover feigned pleasure over my fortune with the kill, but when I pulled up the hem of my cloak and offered the choice meats to the goddess, a green light glinted in his eyes, betraying his anger at being bested.

DURING YET ANOTHER procession out in the Greek provinces, parading past yet another dazzled small town crowd, I spotted a youth fresh in from the countryside, mud and shit still clinging to his boots, a farm boy gawking mouth-open like a fish at all the imperial pageantry. I caught his stare, his frank look of appraisal too innocent to be much abashed by my glance, his demeanor reminding me of Periander, the fish I once let slip back out to sea. That farm boy's thought upon seeing me was captured on his bare face as plain as if he had spoken it aloud:

"You're the one who takes it up the ass every night."

I thought of the blind fox, and smiled.

HADRIAN AND I once again participated in the Eleusinian mysteries. The other initiates, bedecked in myrtle wreaths and golden ribbons, kept a discreet distance while we purified ourselves in the sea, made our sacrifices, and joined the torchlit processional along the ruts of the Sacred Way from Eleusis back to Athens.

Hadrian chose to undergo several other cults' initiations as well, in keeping with the ideals of the new Pantheon back in Rome and his own assumption of a title of deity, Zeus Olympos, to please the Greek citizens under his rule. He had only just accepted the title of Father of the Fatherland from the Roman Senate. He refused the title early in his reign, and said he must earn it (perhaps in emulation of Augustus, who accepted that title only after ruling for twenty-five years).

Some of those cults' rites seemed exotic, to say the least, and others struck us as barbaric, even horrific, such as the ritual castration required as proof of dedication from the priests of Cybele. Hadrian also finds circumcision rites, practiced by some peoples of the Empire, offensive. He said he cannot fathom why such mutilation of the human body is judged seemly, much less holy. Even my initiation into Mithraism sent Hadrian into a spasm of disgust, despite having undergone the ritual himself some years ago.

I shall never forget how steam rose in a wreath from the bull's cut throat before its blood rushed over me in a scalding stream, blinding me momentarily to everything except my own ecstatic vision, the spiritual union of slayer and slain.

Or how, when I emerged from that baptismal pit gory as an infant fresh-sprung from the womb and blinking at the ferocity of the light, I caught a glimpse of Hadrian's face distorted by revulsion, before he reined in that reaction and regained his composure, the impassive mask of Empire slipping into place once more.

I went with him to pay homage at Hector's tomb and at the marble one Hadrian had built to hold the bones of Ajax, where he also sacrificed a golden peacock. I myself made a sacrifice in tribute to Patroclus, friend of Achilles, whose story of devotion I learned in childhood.

While the blood ran and the meat charred, I reflected on all those old stories I drank like mother's milk as a boy. I began to wonder how I missed the real point of those tales of men whose heroism entailed sacrifice for each other: Love requires death to become immortal.

Soon afterward, in an official visit to the barbarian kingdom of Parthia, Hadrian averted further battle and cemented Roman relations with their king, Osroes, by ensuring that a daughter of his, kidnapped by Trajan's forces during an earlier skirmish, was returned. He then allowed the barbarian emperor to take us up into the mountains to hunt deer and hare with leopards and falcons.

AFTER PLOTINA'S DEATH, Hadrian developed an even keener interest in what becomes of the soul at death. This topic engendered several rounds of pillow-talk, for I, too, had given much thought to this matter, recalling the blue butterfly of a ghost which haunted my childhood, the deaths of my father and grandfather, and the Stoic philosopher's rational suicide.

I promised Hadrian that if I died first, I would try to illuminate death for him. He laughed, believing I spoke in jest, but my offer was sincere. Indulging myself in a morbid fancy, I decided I must come back to visit him in the form of a butterfly, blue like my mother, or perhaps as one of the big yellow specimens that hover each summer over a certain weed with straggly white flowers, blooms my grandmother called love-in-ashes.

Not long after that particular conversation, we ventured to the summit of Mount Casius, where Hadrian meant to offer a sacrifice to Zeus after completing the climb.

There atop the peak at first light, just as the priests prepared to offer up the sacrifice, lightning struck, blinding us all for a moment. At once, both an acolyte and the intended sacrifice fell dead before us. Those of us who survived the bolt stood stunned into silence, the air still rent by the scorch of sulphur and flesh burning.

The surviving priests, whose voices shook with awe, proclaimed that both priest and kid had been taken up for the emperor's genius, and the span of their lives added to his, in an acknowledgement by Zeus himself.

Hadrian said nothing, but his arm beneath mine trembled. His health had begun troubling him of late, and the ascent must have fatigued him, but it was not only fatigue that caused his shakiness. I knew he wondered whether he had in truth received a sign of favor, or a portent heralding disaster.

Afterward, he wanted to visit a local seer to determine what such an omen meant, but I declined the opportunity to delve into the future myself. Had I accompanied him, perhaps I might have avoided the disaster that later befell me. Perhaps not.

Arriving in Jerusalem, Hadrian learned that his plan to build a temple to Adonis there had outraged the Jewish people, who demanded that he respect the site of their ruined ancient tabernacle. I fear a crisis will arise from among these people, whose belief in their one god excludes any and all others. Theirs is a zeal only beginning to foment. Their Jehovah is an angry, jealous god; they fear only him, and no other.

Not even a century has passed since nine hundred of their number faced a legion at Masada, beside the Dead Sea, holding off five thousand soldiers for four years. Rather than submit to Rome, they fell upon their own swords by firelight at siege's end. Yet Hadrian seems not to recognize the intransigence of such faith, or else deems it traitorous to the realm of which he is sovereign lord.

We left Judea and followed the coastline down toward Pelusium to begin the long journey to Egypt and Africa. I thought of Calliria. Her words now seemed yet another veiled omen. At Pompey's tomb, Hadrian himself composed an epigram, remarking, "How poor a tomb for one so rich in shrines." He gave orders that it be reclaimed from the sand and restored.

Our initial entry into the land of Egypt went unheralded, a deliberate choice on Hadrian's part. Empress Sabina and Lucius Commodus, though both in ill health, planned to travel to Alexandria with their own parties, including Hadrian's young nephew and possible heir, Pedanius Fuscus. Hadrian chose to delay official festivities until their arrival.

The city of Alexandria received one year's advance notice of our pending visit. Such forewarning is a necessity since the royal entourage requires an enormous amount of provisions, even for a few weeks: a thousand bushels of barley, or about a hundred thousand loaves of bread; three thousand bundles of hay; three hundred suckling pigs; and two hundred sheep.

Sabina's friend Julia Balbilla of Athens, a highly educated poetess, agreed to accompany her on this Egyptian junket. Observing their friendship, I wonder whether the empress is not less lonely than I earlier believed, and I am glad for her in this consolation. Over time, Hadrian's lack of compassion for his wife has begun to grate on me. Odd though it might sound, I would prefer that my consort treat his wife with greater respect and deference than is his habit, for she always has done what was expected of a woman of her station, and cannot help her own awkward nature.

The great city of Alexandria, as cosmopolitan in its way as Rome herself, boasts a veneer of international citizenry over its Greek heritage, set atop the bedrock of the ancients. The Egyptians themselves no longer can decipher the inscriptions with which their ancestors covered their monuments; mysteries lie intact before all eyes, buried within a picture-language which looks at once both familiar and utterly strange.

Hadrian looked forward to examining the tomb of Alexander and visiting the city's museum and library, while I most looked forward to the sights to be found along the Street of the Blessed, and relished the opportunity to study Egyptian religion, with regard to their lion and cat gods and goddesses, Bastet, Sekhmet, Pakhet, Qadesh, Shu, Aker, Mehet, Nefertem, Tefnut, and Edjo, in particular.

During my studies, I also became fascinated by Ammit, "the gobbler," with the head of a crocodile, the front legs of a lion, and the back legs of a hippopotamus (which Herodotus called a river horse). This mythical creature waits beside the balance where the hearts of the deceased are weighed against the Feather of Truth, once they have recited certain spells from the holy Book of the Dead. He eats the hearts of those who wronged others in life.

I felt struck in particular by one incantation from that book, the Negative Confession. It lists many disavowed offenses against one's community, and was written long before, but is quite similar to, the commandments said to have been revealed in stone to Moses and kept by the Jewish tribes: "I have not stolen; I have not coveted; I have not caused another to stumble; I have not given false witness; I have not fornicated; I have not committed murder, I am pure, pure, pure."

And who would designate a scarab, that insect known as the dung-beetle or cockchafer, as a sacred symbol of creation and the sun? The Egyptians.

Even Hadrian was rather taken with their dwarf god Bes, the guardian of home and childbirth. He commissioned a local sculptor to fashion a likeness of the little lion-headed demon-deity for his villa at Tibur.

WE TREKKED OFF into Africa, where for a second time we were to join a lion hunt. Hadrian deemed me old enough to participate at last. One lion in particular, a man-killer, had been causing chaos throughout the region, so Hadrian sought to save his subjects from its ravages. He saved my life on this hunt, as well.

Riding along in the savannah, mountains in the distance shimmering with heat, we talked in a desultory fashion, pointing out sights to one another, such as a colony of termites, an egret startled into flight, unusual rock formations, and some strange red flowers in bloom—the exact shade, I observed to Hadrian, of the crimson wax he employs for leaving his royal mark.

Everything happened so fast.

All at once the man-killer, a tawny mass of muscle and hunger, materialized out of the brush, shaking his enormous dusty head and roaring as if to warn us, turn us back.

Hadrian might have claimed the prize right then, put an end to that day's sport at once with his bronze spear. Instead, he chose only to wound the beast with a blow, leaving its killing to me.

"Take him, Antinous," he shouted at me.

And I—I misjudged the distance between my horse and the thrashing, wounded cat, threw my spear too fast. With both javelins I tried again, but the space had narrowed so that, too close, I could not maneuver for a good throw.

Balius, hunt-trained, battle-hardened, selected with care by my old stable master, stood his ground, not panicking, though his rider sat unarmed and the lion rushed at him. Recalling it now, that horse's valor shames me.

The lion crouched low alongside our flank, meaning to spring against my horse's neck, tear me off and drag me to the ground, but Hadrian, lunging in on Xanthus between the lion and my own mount, struck fast. A terrible roar, and then silence.

All danger past, Hadrian dismounted and motioned for me to come to him, where he stood staring down at the fallen lion. He looked almost as shaken as I felt.

"Antinous, what happened? I cannot—"

He didn't finish the thought. He clasped me to himself in a rough gesture, and I felt his heart charge against the cage of his ribs.

"Thank you," I said, "for saving me. My life is yours."

That night, at a feast which became a frenzy of rejoicing once news of the lion's demise spread, I thanked Hadrian, praising him as we have always praised those heroes of old who offered themselves up for one another.

Neither of us died that day. By his own actions, by his choice, he had put my life at risk. Once again, testing me—I am utterly, fatally convinced of it. Yet he also saved me, and more than ever my life belonged to him, not to me. Already, I knew myself to be lost, trapped, with no hope of escape, while the crows flocked nearer, whispering.

By the time we retired, our guides already had stripped the hide from the beast and cleaned and hoisted that trophy aloft, a grisly memento not unlike the sheet unfurled outside the bridal bower after the wedding night, according to the custom of barbarians (such a sheet might well wind up a shroud if no blood issues forth from the deflowered one). The skin's stench reminded me of the bear pelt Hadrian once sacrificed to Eros, and of another sheet, stained once with my blood.

During the night, he asked if I remembered a lion at the Flavian amphitheatre that had been caged with a canine companion, and how it pined after the dog was taken away, leaving the great beast on its own. I did not remind him how I once employed a lion to chastise him, but perhaps he remembered anyway. He took my face in his hands, searching it in the candlelight.

"Ah, love," he said. "Never die."

A brief fumbling, and then ecstasy. Afterward, I wondered how it could be so simple—rather, why it couldn't always be so.

That night, I began to understand what must be done, but did not yet comprehend how, nor see how such a choice might also serve him, become a gift apart.

NEXT MORNING, RIDING OUT, we saw where the carcass lay cast aside after being skinned, its red and white marbled remains, attended by a host of flies, appearing before us like the foetus of some strange god, a final humiliation for the beast whose scythes had failed to dispatch me.

Hadrian tossed his own mane, the lion conqueror mounted in triumph upon his fine horse, ill health and fear of disaster forgotten. I thought of proud, ruined beauty, Marsyus flayed in porphyry, a grey-eyed bitch cringing before the whip, and my lover, triumphant, playing his flute in the hot breath of the night. I wanted to vomit.

Later, we heard how the locals, claiming to have found a red bloom growing on the spot where the lion fell, renamed the flower after me. Better to have named it after the lion.

BY THE TIME we returned once more to Alexandria, greeted by the gleam of the lighthouse of Pharos, an edifice acclaimed as one of the world's seven wonders, Sabina and Commodus had arrived with their friends and attendants.

Sad news had come from my uncle in Bithynia, by way of the court in Athens, of my grandmother's death. No personal message accompanied the announcement and formal condolences. I knew there would be no more welcome in the house which now belonged to him, after the way he had been humiliated in public by Hadrian's cold reception.

Hadrian, now mindful of his appearance as pharaoh, avoided returning downriver toward Alexandria with the Nile in Akhet, the flood season. The Egyptians believe that to travel on the rising Nile of the flood insults the gods, low though the water remains during this second year of drought. Pharaoh Alexander, in defiance of this sacred edict, once sailed downriver at full flood. Soon afterward, devastated by the loss of his companion Hephaestion, he must have wondered whether the gods of this strange land had indeed punished him for his trespass against the mother river that undulates through this desert country like a green umbilical cord and tethers her people along banks swathed in fecundity.

In the midst of all the pomp and banqueting and official visits undertaken to inspect various sights, Hadrian grew distracted both by his duties and by more agitations fomented by the local Jewish faction over the temple dispute back in Jerusalem. This made my own preoccupation with dishonor after the hunt, and the dilemma of what must be done, easier to conceal from him.

At one point, after fruitless negotiations with an elder from the local synagogue, Hadrian fainted in his quarters, a sign of fatigue or worse. Only a servant and I saw this, and he swore us to secrecy, declining to tell even his physician about the incident.

The next evening, we were taken by boat to visit a magician at Canopus. Once ashore, we were conducted to a dank little grotto of a shop which seemed older than the pyramids themselves and stank of unsavory things. A mummified crocodile's head leered through the gloom as we crossed the threshold into the sorcerer's lair.

There he cast predictions for Hadrian, employing his attendant witch to demonstrate a spell he claimed can attract someone in one hour, send dreams, cause illness in two hours, even destroy a man in seven hours—a spell which he also copied out and sold to Hadrian, who paid him double for it.

The spell calls for a mouse deified in spring water, along with two moon beetles deified in river water. These are to be pounded on a mortar together with a river crab, the fat of a virgin, dappled goat, dung of a dog-faced baboon, two ibis eggs, two drams of storax, two drams of myrrh, two drams of crocus, four drams of Italian galingale, four drams of frankincense, and an onion. This mixture is to be kept in a lead box and used whenever a spell to beseech the goddess is performed, by sprinkling it over a charcoal fire on a rooftop at moonrise. (One must wear a papyrus roll with a protective charm while making the sacrifice as well, according to the sorcerer, lest the goddess make the seeker airborne and then hurl him to the ground.)

Then certain incantations must be spoken over the sacrifice, which vary depending upon one's intentions. For example:

"I offer you this spice, O child of Zeus,
Dart-shooter, Artemis, Persephone,
Shooter of deer, night-shining, triple-sounding,
Triple-voiced, triple-headed Selene,
Triple-pointed, triple-faced, triple-necked,
And goddess of the triple ways, who hold
Untiring flaming fire in triple baskets,
And you who oft frequent the triple way
And rule the triple decades with three forms
And flames and dogs. From toneless throats you send
A dread, sharp cry when you, O goddess, have
Raised up an awful sound with triple mouths.
Hearing your cry, all worldly things are shaken:
The nether gates and Lethe's holy water
And primal Chaos and the shining chasm
Of Tartaros. At it every immortal
And every mortal man, the starry mountains,
Valleys and every tree and roaring rivers,
And even the restless sea, the lonely echo,
And daemons through the world, shudder at you,
O blessed one, when they hear your dread voice.
Come here to me, goddess of night, beast-slayer,
Come and be at my love spell of attraction
Quiet and fruitful, and having your meal
Amid the graves. And heed my prayers, Selene,
Who suffer much, who rise and set at night,
O triple-headed, triple-named Mene
Marzoune, fearful, gracious-minded, and

Persuasion. Come to me, horned-face, light-bringer,
Bull-shaped, horse-faced goddess, who howl doglike;
Come here, she-wolf, and come here now, Mistress
Of night and chthonic realms, holy, black-clad,
'Round whom the star-traversing nature of
The world revolves whenever you wax too great.
You have established every worldly thing,
For you engendered everything on earth
And from the sea and every race in turn
Of winged birds who seek their nests again.
Mother of all, who bore Love, Aphrodite,
Lamp-bearer, shining and aglow, Selene,
Star-coursing, heavenly, torch-bearer, fire-breather,
Woman four-faced, four-named, four-roads' mistress.
Hail, goddess, and attend your epithets,
O heavenly one, harbor goddess, who roam
The mountains, are goddess of the crossroads;
O nether one, goddess of depths, eternal,
Goddess of dark, come to my sacrifices.
Fulfill for me this task, and as I pray
Give heed to me, Lady, I ask of you."

This, to attract love. (To ask the goddess to punish a slanderer, or any other who has given offense, the incantations become much graver.)

This same sorcerer also offered to make a certain special sacrifice for the emperor's genius. Hadrian made it clear no human sacrifice was acceptable in honoring him. Still, I absorbed every particular as the magician described the requirements for this ceremony, which seems to me in keeping with the Roman generals' own time-honored practice of devotio suicide. It reminded me as well of the voluntary sacrifice of the Nazarene of the Christians' sect, who was crucified, then deified, one hundred years ago. Such rites call for a subject willing to give up one life for another.

Egyptian custom calls for this particular sacrifice to be drowned in the Nile's waters, in order to be assimilated unto Osiris, god of the dying and resurrected. The sorcerer told us the pharaoh's genius may afterward assume the form of such a sacrifice, to appear to him and serve him in the future. The Egyptians' official mourning festival to honor the death of Osiris having just begun, any such sacrifices now offered are considered particularly effective.

When I asked the sorcerer if any animal sacrifice might make an acceptable substitute, he allowed that the voluntary sacrifice of a pet might suffice. I then volunteered to offer up the falcon of Osroene, a gift from the mountain king to Hadrian, who later in turn gave it to me, amused by my fascination with the creature, its glowering amber eyes and downy breast. The least I could do, to offer it back to him.

Once the courier returned from fetching it, a sorceress performed the rites in preparation for the sacrifice. She removed the small leather head covering which kept the bird soothed, but by some means of enchantment soon lulled it back into sleep. The sorcerer observed that it is crucial for the victim of this rite to appear to have volunteered for the sacrifice, not to have struggled with death.

She anointed the falcon, then with one swift thrust immersed its motionless body in a vat of holy water drawn from the Nile, cradling it in her hands, tender as any mother, until the river stilled the heart and unsheathed the spirit, allowing it to fly to Osiris and become one with Hadrian's genius.

Hadrian paid the chief sorcerer in gold, and then our party returned to the boat to be ferried back to the city.

MARCELLUS ONCE TOLD me the Egyptians must deify anyone, prince or commoner, who happens to drown in the Nile, as one chosen by Osiris and Isis. They believe the taboo against suicide is lifted, too, from all of those claimed by the Great Mother. He said the local legends do not agree with Plutarch's claim that a fish swallowed Osiris' penis (oh innocent red fish); the Egyptians believe his phallus still resides in Memphis.

As one might expect, Marcellus also became fascinated with the embalming ritual the Egyptians practice, a desiccation procedure, and expressed a hope that he might someday be allowed to observe such a ceremony.

I meant to share with him what I saw in these various Egyptian rituals and ceremonies, and also what I learned about the cat and lion deities worshipped here, which constitute quite a pantheon among themselves: Sekhmet and Bastet, daughter and eye of Re, are givers of healing and power; Edjo and Pakhet guard entrances, south and east; Qadeshis is a goddess offering sacred and sexual ecstasy; Shu rules over air; Tefnut over moisture; Aker over earth, guarding the east and west horizons of the underworld; Mehet is responsible for the flooding of the Nile; Nefertem of the primeval lotus blossom symbolizes new life and re-creation, and Bes, of course, presides over birth.

Studying the beliefs of these people, I recall once more those deepest cave-fears, those which haunt one forever—and here at last, find a voice from the fire to illuminate the cave, to speak out over the bones:

Be still, Antinous, and listen.

One may think one has grasped the concept of Empire. But not until we arrived in this alien land and encountered these strangers, who believe that our emperor, like their pharaohs before him, is a god incarnate, did I begin to comprehend the truth of it. The well-being of entire races, countless souls in provinces numerous as butterflies in a meadow, depends on the understanding and judicious use of power by the one man who wields it over all.

No military conqueror or expansionist, Hadrian has chosen to fortify the empire's borders, improve relations with allied kingdoms, restore and expand public services, and commission new works of art for the cultural enhancement of the empire. It was his idea that slaves must no longer be sold as gladiators to the combat schools, since unlike freedmen they have no choice in the matter. He also means to outlaw the mutilations practiced by those who circumcise their infants, though this act is practiced as a ritual of devotion by the Jewish community, and his ban may cause further revolts.

Hadrian is a staunch proponent of the Roman Peace, and the coins of our realm are inscribed with his philosophy: Humanitas, Libertas, Felicitas.

Yet how can one who has absolute power, who has always had power, ever begin to imagine being one who has no power? I wonder.

Meanwhile, I have grown disenchanted to the point of disgust with Commodus, the heir-apparent, whose extravagance here with his entourage strikes me as obscene, seeing how these people suffer from the drought, estranged from their Nile who has withheld her brown, stinking love for two seasons now.

How can anyone look into their faces, eyes engorged with hunger and fear as they stagger through the eternal red dust alongside their camels and bony oxen, and not realize how these people are suffering. The peasants in the furrows work and starve, no better off than slaves, so that the grain harvested from this land may pour into the coffers of Rome. Meanwhile, our imperial retinue is plied with dates and pomegranates.

The Egyptians' pyramids, monuments inscribed with the tongue of the dead, built to commemorate kings gone for ages before Rome existed, serve as a mirror and metaphor for society: Glorification of the elect few, raised to a pinnacle above and supported by a base of countless souls existing in misery.

Yet Commodus chats on, oblivious, about flower gardens, peacocks and scarabs, what subtle new colors the dye maker has promised for the fall. Just like Marcus back in Rome, he protects his complexion from the vicious sun with a flour mask, his face a cake studded with raisin eyes and nostrils and a red currant mouth.

Some wag of the court—probably Favorinus—has dubbed Commodus the Western favorite, myself the Eastern favorite, and these nicknames are now all the fashion; I fear, although we sojourn in the east, the west may triumph, ascendant. Pancrates, obsequious pander of a poet, also seized the chance to further laurel

Hadrian by promising an epic in verse to commemorate this last lion hunt, equating it with Herakles' slaying of the Nemean lion. I suppose it never occurred to either of them to wonder, or care, whether I might wish not to be memorialized as the one who could not save himself, equated with that hero's companion, Hylas, drowned when adoring water nymphs pulled him down into a spring.

Patrician Commodus may be, but I cannot fathom how Hadrian could consider him as successor. Commodus seems not even to notice how tired and strained our emperor looks now beneath the royal headdress with its uraeus, a rearing cobra that spits at the pharaoh's enemies. Hadrian knows these people look to him for divine assistance, yet even he cannot end the drought, or coax the Nile to flood again.

DAYS AGO, WHEN we were allowed upon the Nile at last, we passed upriver by Heliopolis, ruins of the city of the sun, and home of the phoenix. I hoped then that my old love for Hadrian, and his for me, might rise again from the ashes. I offered to stay in the temple of Serapis for him, a practice the Egyptians claim can send healing dreams from a god or goddess through the sleep of the intermediary. He declined, saying he preferred to keep me by his side. But I cannot stay there forever.

In another month, in this Fifteenth Year of Hadrian Caesar Our Lord, I myself shall turn nineteen. I hang suspended now between childhood and manhood, and soon must go to ground.

Now I see all too well how my lost inheritance might have provided a softer landing, allowed for independence and a measure of dignity when my time arrives to be cast aside. My lover, wiser, foresaw this problem with clarity; this accounted in part for his fury against my uncle. Whereas I, in my prime, gave no more thought than Icarius, or Phaeton in the chariot of the sun, to the eventual reality of descent. Now comes my turn to fall.

Every day the truth I must confront gnaws deeper into my vitals, like the fox hidden beneath the Lacedaemonian boy's tunic: Hadrian is the master of every man's destiny, down to the lowest slave in Rome, whereas I cannot even become the master of my own.

Once I believed our life together represented a great love, like the heroes of old, the bonds of the Sacred Band. Instead, it is about power and control. Hadrian holds all that power, always has, and always will.

Filled with anger, self-disgust, I torment myself. *Kneel, dog. Lie down at the feet of your master. Kiss his hand and lick his heel to acknowledge your submission.*

When the time comes, when our relationship becomes inappropriate because of my facial hair, when the offering of a coin is made to Lady Juventas in thanks for my new white toga, he will discard me with no qualm, as a girl casts an outgrown doll into the river, or a peasant smashes an idol which no longer inspires awe. While back in Rome waits a whole new crop of beautiful boys to comfort him.

As emperor, Hadrian has no choice. He must put me away or look ridiculous; and I, pathetic. But for me to choose in turn another, younger lover—my right, upon becoming a man—would appear disloyal, even traitorous.

I cannot imagine what life might be after life in the court of Hadrian. I can summon only disjointed images:

A fly buzzing over an empty cradle; sun falling on a cracked vase the color of water; an old man walking, lost in the dust of his thoughts.

So I, a citizen, now find I have less freedom to choose an honorable life than any barbarian woman; unmanned, like a priest of Cybele, by the one I have worshipped.

But poets and philosophers tell us love conquers all, even death—since death becomes the lover of all. Eros is not mocked; let us worship the god of love.

HADRIAN HAS GONE to dine already. I must put this scroll aside for now and join everyone at supper, or my absence will cause speculation. My behavior this evening must be exemplary, my gaiety unforced. A final night of merriment seems fitting. Sabina and Julia Balbilla look forward to their visit to the Colossi of Memnon (one of which, it is said, serenades his mother, Eos Aurora, while her tears linger on the ground at dawn). I regret I cannot share this adventure. I would have liked to hear such singing.

The river laps at the boat like a lazy brown dog, and rising unstifled by the heat outside Hermopolis, a lullaby. How many evenings now we have been serenaded thus, urged toward slumber by a stranger's voice.

I will wear a new outfit, look festive, and finish this last chapter late in the night, while my lover, sated, lies sleeping.

WATER

IV. Water

A GLORIOUS SKY, bristling with stars. Whispers have emerged among local astronomers of a strange alignment soon to take place in the heavens—a new star, hidden, in waiting, soon will make its presence known.

Such a quiet night, after Alexandria. I can hear the wild dogs barking along the banks outside Hermopolis, where the imperial flotilla lies anchored. Farther down, ibis and river horse alike doze hidden among reeds beneath the turning wheel of constellations. The moon itself is dark, an auspicious sign for my purposes.

Here in our quarters, the only other soul awake is the guard on watch. Should he come round to check, these words are safe—he cannot read Greek. These last four nights, while the empire sleeps, I have assigned myself this confession. Any struggle must be resolved here upon these sheets, so the morrow holds nothing but acceptance, acquiescence, peace. With this lamp as witness I record my life until now. When I am finished, I must consign it all, save the final chapter, to the temple fire.

Earth, air, fire, water—all elements must be in accord for Our Lady to accept my offering for Hadrian's genius. That confluence of elements approaches.

I have watched my last sunset, and await my final sunrise. This animal, my body, cannot comprehend my mind, does not anguish or fight like a bull or a kid led to slaughter. How odd, how precious, is life.

WHAT I MUST wear tomorrow.

Nothing elaborate, lest clothes call attention to the deed. If he becomes suspicious, he will have me followed, try to stop me. I must slip away when he is distracted. Renouncing love this way relieves him of the burden of doing so.

I suppose I will soil myself. The body voids itself at death. We come from nothing, pray to nothing, and dying return to nothing. Thus we achieve perfection.

SOMETHING SOFT, AND shimmering, and pure.

The current will be merciful enough to wash any filth away. Perhaps, once arrived, I will set my garment aside on the shore, along with the ankh amulet, life-giving water sign like a man with his arms spread wide, which Hadrian gave me. I may steal one of the kerchiefs I gave him, and carry that down as well. Then he will know I carried the essence of him away with me.

HERE ON THESE pages I have tried to write the truth. But it changes like the wind, blowing across the stone of fact, first from this direction, now from that, and no one wind is more or less real than another, no more or less true than that around which it dances and moans. I can only attest to my own version.

I AM ALMOST nineteen. I have studied, traveled, beheld the wonders of the empire. All my lover asked in return was that I give myself to him—body, mind, and soul. For seven years I belonged to him, faithful as his favorite sight hound, obedient as his strongest boar-baiter. What other choice does any dog have. Fucker.

The sorcerer assured me such a sacrifice will bring glory to the emperor's genius and add decades to his life. His genius now a priest, kid, falcon, butterfly.

WHEN THIS NEW suitor embraces her, may the Nile restore her bounty to her children once again, and they in turn lift the emperor on waves of gratitude.

May she come back to them, may she come back, embrace everyone with swirl, eddy, cascade upon flood. Raise hands unto Isis, great goddess. Sing all her names in praise. Some perhaps may trouble even to learn this latest lover's name, and so let it live again, conjoined with hers upon their lips.

THE PAIN WILL not last. I do not fear it. No death could hurt like the death-in-life I am rejecting. The beast will kick by instinct—but my will is stronger. I must return to the Great Mother's womb, let my lungs drink their fill of her. Goddess, grant your son the courage of the lion, that he may adore you forever.

THIS IS A kinder fate, chosen by my own hand, than any my lover might mete, no matter how noble his intention. This death honors him, serves his genius, but its agency is mine. At last I reclaim my own, my birthright as a Greek and citizen of Rome, and repay Hadrian for my life.

PERICLES SAID ACTS deserve acts in their honor, not mere words; and a final act of devotion, such as the sacrifice of those who fell for Athens, is justly measured against all of one's other acts in a lifetime.

Therefore,

Imperator Caesar Trajan Hadrian Augustus
Ruler of the civilized world and guardian of the Roman peace
—lover master father brother slave—
I who am about to die salute you, and offer up this vow of sacrifice:
I will go down to the temple, cremate this offering, recite a prayer
I will go down to the river, anointed with attar, step into the water
I will go down to the bed of the Nile, embrace both Isis and Osiris
I will go down to the House of Death, walk in the Elysian Fields
I will go down
I will
I

AFTERWORD

THE ROMAN EMPEROR Hadrian, devastated by the loss of his lover Antinous in 130 CE, would comment only, "He fell into the Nile." Rumor abounded due to the emperor's grief, which many contemporaries deemed excessive, and also due to the circumstances surrounding the youth's demise. Historians of the day noted that Hadrian "cried like a woman" over the death of his beloved.

Hadrian had Antinous deified, an honor reserved for members of the imperial family, and after his beloved's apotheosis appointed a temple and devised rites for the cult of Antinous. He also commissioned the building of a Greek city, Antinöopolis, along the bank of the Nile, near the site where the body was found. After recovery, the body was embalmed according to Egyptian custom, although the final burial site of Antinous is unknown. Some speculate that he was interred on the grounds of Hadrian's villa at Tibur.

Hadrian commissioned numerous likenesses of Antinous by various sculptors and painters, carrying his favorites along during his travels. Hadrian survived the youth he loved until his own death of natural causes at age sixty-two in 138 CE.

Remnants of the Antinous cult remained extant all over the Roman Empire for several hundred years after his death—far longer than Hadrian's own official cult survived—although later historians, in particular those affiliated with the early Christian church, vilified him. St. Athanasius, writing in 350 CE, described him as a "shameless and scandalous boy," "Hadrian's minion," and "wretch," and the "sordid and loathsome instrument of his master's lust."

Numerous sculptures and other art works portraying Antinous, the youth who became a god, still may be found in museums around the world, including the Vatican.

APPENDICES

Appendix I: Dialogue of Hadrian and Epictetus (Questions and Answers)

"What is gold?"
"The purchase of death."
"What is silver?"
"The place of envy."
"What is iron?"
"The implement of all arts."
"What is that which man is not able to see?"
"Another heart."
"By what thing do men err?"
"Cupidity."
"What is liberty?"
"Innocence."
"What is the best, and indeed, the worst?"
"A word."
"What is a man?"
"Similar to a bath: The first room is the tepidarium, the warm bath, in which infants are born thoroughly anointed; the second room, the sudatorium, the

sweat-room, is boyhood; the third room is the assa, the dry-room, the preference of youth; the fourth room, the frigidarium, the cold bath, is appropriate to old age, in which sense comes to all."

"What is a man?"

"Similar to a fruit: Fruits that hang on trees, thus even are our bodies: when ripe they fall, or else they become embittered."

"What is a man?"

"As a lamp placed in the wind."

"What is a man?"

"A stranger of place, the image of law, a tale of calamity, a slave of death, the delay of life; that with which Fortune would frequently make its own game."

"What is heaven?"

"The summit of boundlessness."

"What is heaven?"

"The atmosphere of the world."

"What are stars?"

"The destiny of humans."

"What are stars?"

"The omens of navigators."

"What is the sea?"

"The way of doubt."

"What is a boat?"

"A wandering house."

"What is sleep?"

"An image of death."

"What is love?"

"The annoyance of heart's leisure, shamefulness in boys, reddening in virgins, fury in women, ardor in youth, laughter in age, it is worthlessness in the mocking of fault."

"What is god?"

"That which maintains all things."

"What is a sacrifice?"

"A lessening."

"What is without fellowship?"

"Kingship."

"What is a king?"

"A piece of the gods."

"What is Rome?"

"The fount of authority of the sphere of the earth, mother of nations, possessor of things, the common-dwelling of the Romans, consecration of eternal peace."

"What is that which is pleasing to some and displeasing to others?"

"Life."

"What is the best life?"

"The shortest one."

"What thing is most certain?"

"Death."

"What is death?"

"Perpetual security."

"What is death?"

"The fearing of many, if the wise man lives, inimical to life, the spirit of the living, the dread of parents, the spoils of freedom, the cause of testaments, the conversation after destruction, the end of woefulness, the forgetfulness after memory, the leading torch, the load of burial, the inscription of a monument; death is the end of all evil."

Appendix II: Secundus Commenting on Hadrian

"You, too, Hadrian, are a human being like all the rest of us, subject to every kind of accident, mere dust and corruption. . .

"But you, Hadrian, as it happens, are full of fears and apprehensions. In the bellowing wind of winter you are disturbed too much by cold and shivering, and in the summer time you are too much oppressed by the heat. You are puffed up and full of holes, like a sponge. For you have termites in your body and herds of lice, that draw furrows through your entrails; and grooves have been burned into you, as it were, like the lines made by the fire of encaustic painters. Being a short-lived creature and full of infirmities, you foresee yourself being cut and torn apart, roasted by the sun and chilled by the wintry wind. Your laughter is only the preface to grief, for it turns about and passes into tears. . .

"Boast not that you alone have encircled the world in your travels, for it is only the sun and the moon and the stars that really make the journey around it. Moreover, do not think of yourself as being beautiful and great and rich and the ruler of the inhabited world. Know you not that, being a man, you were born to be Life's plaything, helpless in the hands of Fortune and Destiny, sometimes exalted, sometimes humbled lower than the grave?"

Appendix III: Second Sibylline Oracle, from Phlegon's Book of Marvels

"In my divinely-fashioned loom, and with multicolored weavings

Let holy Ploutonis be adorned, that there be a check against evils.

That which is most beautiful and wished for on earth

For mortals to see, let it be carried zealously

To the royal maiden as a gift mixed with the loom.

And when you pray to Demeter and pure Persephone

To ward off the yoke from your land forever,

Offer to Aidoneus Plouton the blood of a dark-haired ox

Attired in splendid garments, with the help of a herdsman, who

Trusting in the oracle's purpose will slaughter the ox

In the company of all other men in the land who trust in its purpose.

Let no disbeliever be present at the sacrifices,

But let him rather stand apart where it is customary for disbelievers to be,

And perform a sacrifice that is not eaten.

But whoever comes to it knowing our oracle,

Let him seek out holy lord Phoibos in sacrifices,

Zealously burning rich thigh-bones on his altars,

Sacrificing the youngest of the bright goats. And, you know,

Let the suppliant garland his head and beseech Phoibos Paieon

For a release from the evil that is impending,

And when he returns from this, let him beseech royal mistress Hera,

Sacrificing a white cow according to the ancestral custom in the land. . .

I covered my lovely eyes with my veil when I picked
Glorious leaves of the fruitful grey olive-tree. . .
Let them establish an image of holy Queen Hera
And a temple in the ancestral manner.
The evil will come—if you do all this and trust in my words,
Going to the most holy queen with sacrifices and
Performing the wineless rites for as many days as there
are in the year,
Long and into the future—but not in your time.
The man who does this will have power forever."

Appendix IV: Astrological Information for Antinous and Hadrian

The ancients were fascinated with the constellations and astrology. In his *Astronomica*, Marcus Manilius recorded his theories on the signs of the zodiac, the twelve unmoving temples (houses), and instructions for calculating horoscopes, for both individuals and countries (for example, Italy was considered to be governed by Libra, Greece by Virgo).

With Hadrian's horoscope having survived in manuscript form, it is known that he was born with the Sun, Moon, and Jupiter in Aquarius, Saturn and Mercury in Capricorn, and Venus and Mars in Pisces. An astrologist's interpretation would reveal an individual who was ambitious, preoccupied with power, arrogant, stubborn, and with a strong sense of justice, while in personal relationships, inclined to be ruled by emotion. Those with the moon in Aquarius also were considered to have a flair for astrology. (Hadrian was, in fact, interested in the practice.)—from www.meta-religion.com.

According to practicing astrologist Vicki Dickens, if Antinous was indeed nineteen at the time of his death, as some sources believe, he would have been born with the Moon in Cancer, Mercury and Mars in Scorpio, Venus and Jupiter in Capricorn, and Saturn in Pisces, with Sagittarius ascendant. If born on November 27, 111 AD, he may have been Aquarius rising, with the Moon in Taurus and the Sun in Sagittarius. These signs would indicate an independent, original thinker, likeable but capable of remaining aloof; one whose romantic nature inclined toward ardent, impulsive, devoted behavior.

These two individuals' readings taken together would indicate a couple who were compatible, if volatile, within a highly charged emotional and sexual relationship.

There is no easy way to the stars from Earth.

—Seneca

ACKNOWLEDGMENTS

THANKS TO MY publisher, Seriously Good Books, and my editor, Vinnie Kinsella. Thanks to Ellery Harvey for the book design and layout, and artist Megan Chapman for the ravishing cover photo.

Thanks to Hawthornden International Retreat for Writers for a 2008 Fellowship granted for *Eromenos*; to Vermont Studio Center for a 2002 residency; eternal thanks to Sue Kennington for three residencies at her home in Tuscany with Mimi and the boys, and thanks to Kim Alter and Vincent Dawans for letting me hang out in Portland, OR.

Thanks to Marian George, Victoria Costello, Anne Korkeakivi, Kim Alter, Allison Wolcott, Louise Farmer Smith, Fiona Mackintosh, and Gimbiya Kettering for manuscript readings and encouragement. Thanks to Vicki Dickens, who cast a horoscope for Antinous. Thanks to all of my teachers and fellow students in the creative writing program at the University of Arkansas, most especially Joanne Meschery, who directed my thesis. Thanks to Drs. Johnny and Susan Wink, English professors and inspirations. Love and thanks to friends, family, Sean, and Mom, for their love and encouragement.

Most of all, my love and gratitude to Kevin.

Permissions and Quotations:

The opening Catullus quotation, Epigram 85, is from *Eros the Bittersweet* by Anne Carson (Champaign, IL: Dalkey Archive Press, 2003), p. 6.

The quoted poems by Florus and Hadrian are from *Following Hadrian: A Second-Century Journey Through the Roman Empire* by Elizabeth Speller (New York, NY: Oxford University Press, paperback, 2004), p. 83.

The quotation by Secundus regarding Hadrian is from *Life of Secundus the Philosopher*, translated by Ben Edwin Perry, monograph *Historia de Segundo*, American Philological Association (Ithaca, NY: Cornell University Press, 1964), no. 22.

The dialogue of Hadrian and Epictetus is from *Altercatio Hadriani Augusti et Epicteti Philosophi*, translated in *The Phillupic Hymns* by P. Sufenas Virius Lupus (Eugene, OR: Bibliotheca Alexandrina, 2008), pp. 233-237, with notes on p. 271.

The symptoms and treatment of lycanthropy are from *On Lycanthropy* by Marcellus Sidetes, translated by Daniel Ogden in *Magic, Witchcraft, and Ghosts in the Greek and Roman Worlds: A Sourcebook* (New York, NY: Oxford University Press, paperback 2002), pp. 185-186, Ch. 8, Section 142.

The quotes regarding the physiognomy of Favorinus and of Hadrian are from *De Physiognomica by Polemo of Smyrna*, translated by Maud W. Gleason in *Making*

Men: Sophists and Self-Presentation in Ancient Rome (Princeton, NJ: Princeton University Press, 1995), p. 7 and p. 45.

The quotations on hunting dogs are from *On Hunting with Hounds* by Arrian of Bithynia, translated by Malcolm M. Willcock, in *Xenophon and Arrian on Hunting*, ed. A.A. Phillips and Malcolm M. Willcock (Wiltshire, UK: Aris & Phillips Ltd.), section 5.1-6 and sections 33-34.

The spell from the *Egyptian Book of the Dead* is a brief paraphrase based on the *Negative Confessions from the Papyrus of Ani*, used in ancient Egyptian preparations for the afterlife, from the *Book of the Dead*, translated by Sir E.A. Wallis Budge, British Mus. No. 10477, Sheet 22.

The spell by the magician in Egypt is paraphrased from a spell called "Pancrates' Spell for Hadrian," translated by Hans Dieter Betz in *The Greek Magical Papyri in Translation including the Demotic Spells, Volume One: Texts, Second Edition* (Chicago, IL: University of Chicago Press, 1996), pp. 82-85.

I also want to note the following works, which provided inspiration and information during the research and writing of this novel:

Memoirs of Hadrian, a novel by Marguerite Yourcenar; *Beloved and God: The Story of Hadrian and Antinous* by Royston Lambert; *Hadrian: The Restless Emperor* by Anthony R. Birley; *The Mirror of the Self: Sexuality, Self-Knowledge, and the Gaze in the Early Roman Empire* by Shadi Bartsch; *Sexuality in Greek and Roman Culture* by Marilyn B. Skinner; *The History of Sexuality, Vol. I, An Introduction* by Michel Foucault; *The History of Sexuality,*

Vol. II, The Use of Pleasure by Michel Foucault; *Men in Love: Male Homosexualities from Ganymede to Batman* by Vittorio Lingiardi, M.D.; *Bisexuality in the Ancient World* by Eva Cantarella; *Greek Homosexuality* by K.J. Dover; *Dionysos: Archetypal Image of Indestructible Life* by Carl Kerenyi; *Sailing the Wine-Dark Sea: Why the Greeks Matter* by Thomas Cahill; *Phaedrus by Plato*, translated by Christopher Rowe; *Dialogues of Plato (The Jowett Translations)*, edited by Justin D. Kaplan; *Plato and Platonism* by Walter Pater; *The Greek Philosophers* by Rex Warner; *Life in Ancient Rome* by F.R. Cowell; *Handbook to Life in Ancient Rome* by Lesley Adkins and Roy A. Adkins; *Daily Life in Ancient Rome* by Jerome Carcopino; *The Oxford History of the Roman World*, edited by John Boardman, Jasper Griffin and Oswyn Murray; *The Ancient City: Life in Classical Athens and Rome* by Peter Connolly and Hazel Dodge; *Travel in the Ancient World* by Lionel Casson; *The Greek Way, The Roman Way*, and *Mythology* by Edith Hamilton; *Bulfinch's Mythology* modern abridgment by Edmund Fuller; *Caesar Against the Celts* by Ramon L. Jimenez; *Ancient Egypt* by Lorna Oakes and Lucia Gahlin; *Apologia Contra Arianos*, St. Athanasius, ca. 350 AD (Parker translation, 1713), and *Dio's Rome, Volume V, Book 69* by Cassius Dio (Project Gutenberg EBooks).

QUESTIONS FOR READERS' GROUP DISCUSSIONS:

1. Though a member of the Imperial Court of Rome, Antinous was Greek. How might his nationality have affected his perceptions of Roman culture?

2. What effect did class differences have on Antinous' relationships with other students at the Imperial School? What effect did they have on his relationship with Emperor Hadrian?

3. How would Antinous' coming of age—"taking on the white toga"—impact his relationship with Hadrian?

4. In what ways were Roman society's perceptions and assumptions about homosexuality similar to those of contemporary society? In what ways might these perceptions and assumptions differ from those of today?

5. Controversy still exists today over whether the actual death of Antinous was a murder, a suicide, or an accident. How does the author of this novel choose to portray his death? What incidents in the novel might be seen as factors that contribute to the character's choice to sacrifice himself in devotio suicide?

About the Author

Melanie McDonald won a 2008 Hawthornden Fellowship for *Eromenos*. She has an MFA in fiction from the University of Arkansas. Her work has appeared in *New York Stories, Fugue, Indigenous Fiction,* and online. She has pursued the craft of writing in New York, Galway, Paris, and in Italy while at work on this novel. An Arkansas native, she now lives in Virginia with her husband, Kevin McDonald, author of *Above the Clouds: Managing Risk in the World of Cloud Computing.*

Made in the USA
Middletown, DE
16 September 2016